A Blurred
Reality

ROY LEWIS

A Blurred Reality

An Eric Ward novel

St. Martin's Press
New York

A BLURRED REALITY. Copyright © 1985 by Roy Lewis. All rights reserved. Printed in the United States of America. No part of this book may be used or reproduced in any manner whatsoever without written permission except in the case of brief quotations embodied in critical articles or reviews. For information, address St. Martin's Press, 175 Fifth Avenue, New York, N.Y. 10010.

Library of Congress Cataloging in Publication Data

Lewis, Roy, 1933–
   A blurred reality.

   I. Title.
PR6062.E954B5   1985   823'.914   85-12529
ISBN 0-312-08725-X

First published in Great Britain by William Collins Sons & Co. Ltd.

First U.S. Edition

10 9 8 7 6 5 4 3 2 1

A Blurred
Reality

CHAPTER 1

1

Two men sat quietly in the dark blue car and waited.

In front of them the hill slipped away, the streets lurching raggedly down towards the river, grey roofs gleaming dully after the light rain that had fallen. Across the river, on the north bank of the Tyne, a stray gleam of late afternoon sunshine picked out a bright reflection from the windows of the old flour mill at Dunston, while near the Redheugh jetty a small tanker manoeuvred, sliding away from the coal staiths where barges had once tied up for loading.

'High tide,' said the man with the scarred nose.

His companion grunted and lit a cigarette, shielding the match's flare against the light breeze that fluttered in through the open window. He drew on the cigarette reflectively, narrowing his eyes against the smoke. The knot of people along the roadway fifty yards ahead was thinning.

The man with the scarred nose shifted his bulk impatiently, eager to end the inactivity of the last fifteen minutes. He was not used to sitting still for long, and his heavy, broken-knuckled hands kneaded at his thighs as his glance moved over the collection of women milling near the school gates. Some of them were walking away now, clutching small children by the hand; others were in small groups, talking, children waiting beside them as the grown-ups used the late-afternoon opportunity to socialize.

The senior school was beginning to spill out, older youngsters emerging from the red-brick building to walk past the Victorian tarmacadam yard of the junior school and make their way into the road. A few cars, elderly and battered in the main, stood waiting to swallow some of them; others wandered in little groups up the hill, and down the hill and across the road into the streets that fanned out from the school.

The minutes ticked by and the heavy hands kneaded away. The schoolchildren was thinning, the noise they made lessening, and some of the cars parked near the school had gone, the others now preparing to go. The man with the scarred nose cleared his throat. 'Any sign yet?'

The man behind the wheel ground out his cigarette stub in the ashtray and nodded. 'Just there.' As his companion craned forward he added impatiently, 'Take it easy. Look, just behind that youngster with the red anorak.'

She was about thirteen years old. She was dressed neatly in formal school uniform: white blouse, navy blue jacket, dark blue skirt. Her hair was fair, cut short, curling, and her face seemed pale as she stood with her back against the wall beside the school entrance. She remained quite still, talking to no one, her hands in front of her, fingers interlaced. She glanced down the hill every few seconds, as though watching for someone to come; otherwise, she kept her gaze lowered, staring blankly at the roadway in front of her.

An older girl came strolling through the school gates. Taller, more confident, she had dispensed with school formality and wore a patterned skirt slightly too small for her, a light-coloured sweater that emphasized her early maturity. She carried an anorak slung carelessly over one shoulder and she said something to the waiting thirteen-year-old. There was only a brief reply; it caused the older girl to push the younger in annoyance. Then she walked away, pausing uncertainly at the kerb before she glanced up the hill towards the waiting car. She hesitated for a few seconds more and then, casually, began to walk up the hill.

The man with the scarred nose grunted deep in his throat.

The shaft of sunlight broadened, warming the Newcastle bank and changing the colour of the dark river. The last of the cars outside the school made their turns, chugged away home and the girl at the gates waited patiently, fingers laced, still contemplating the roadway. The older girl neared the blue car in which the two men sat. The broken-knuckled hands tensed, stubby fingers slightly bent. The guttural throat noise came again, half-pleasure, half-warning.

The girl came on, her stride slowing but lengthening to change the swing of her hip, introduce a deliberate sensuality into her walk. She raised her hand to adjust the anorak on her shoulder and held the pose, elbow lifted, raising the line of her sweater, tightening against the breast. She had blue eyes, wide, deliberately innocent yet deep with knowledge. She came forward, touched the bonnet of the car, slid slim, soft fingers along the radio aerial, and smiled. 'Hi.'

The man behind the wheel ignored her. His companion tensed momentarily but then relaxed his stubby fingers. The girl's smile widened and she slid forward slightly, her fingers still holding the aerial. 'You are looking for someone?'

'No.'

It was the man behind the wheel who spoke, a hint of impatience already staining his tone.

'Maybe *waiting* for someone, then.' She released the aerial and came to stand beside the open window of the car. Her fingers rested on the car door; the man with the scarred nose looked at them, then raised his eyes to the girl's. 'I mean,' she said tentatively, 'why wait?'

There was a car chugging its way up the hill. It was a ten-year-old green Morris, its bulbous body rust-scarred, its elderly engine wheezing a complaint against the steepness of the slope. It held three people: a woman, and two children. Gears clashed as the woman failed to gauge the slope correctly; the vehicle lurched, then gathered speed again as it pulled towards the school gates.

The young girl at the entrance unlaced her fingers.

In the dark blue car the man behind the wheel grunted and looked at his watch, checking the time carefully. His companion in the passenger seat shifted, his eyes level with the breasts of the girl at the car door, his fingers tensing again.

The girl in the light-coloured sweater tossed her head,

dark hair swirling past her mouth, pale-lipsticked, a hasty
addition as she had left the school buildings. 'I can show
you a good time. Good as any in the West End.' She leaned
forward, her dark head close to the window, and the man
with the scarred nose could see the coarseness of her young
skin, a pitting along the cheek, marks of youthful acne
around her camouflaged mouth. 'Believe me,' she whispered
gutturally, in a near-parody of sexual invitation.

Down at the school gates the green Morris had turned in
the roadway, pulled up at the entrance and the car door
was opening. The thirteen-year-old was getting into the
Morris. Above them, on the hill, the man behind the wheel
of the dark blue car started the engine.

'Where you going?' the girl in the light sweater said
quickly. 'I'm in no hurry. You want to take me along? I can
show you—'

'Go away, little girl,' the man behind the wheel said
shortly.

'Ho, you got it wrong, mister,' the girl said confidently.
Her fingers fastened on the car door. 'There's nothing *little*
about me, you know what I mean? I'm *experienced*, and if
you treat me right, I'm not fussy, you know what I mean,
pet?' Her tone took on a whining, pleading note. 'Come on,
what's your hurry? I know a place up at High Team where
you can—'

The car engine roared. The man with the scarred nose
lifted a hand, fastened on the girl's fingers, pinning them to
the door. She yelped with pain as the grip intensified,
bruising her fingers against the metal. The car began to
inch forward and she was forced to stagger beside it, all
sexuality suddenly gone as the car picked up speed; she was
forced to run, and fear scored across her sagging mouth.

'For God's sake—'

The man with the scarred nose gripped hard, digging his
fingers into the bone of the wrist, making sure the bruise
would remind her for days. He spoke, for the first time.
'Now bugger off, you little whore!'

He released her hand and she lurched back as the car
gained speed, thrusting away from the kerb. She screamed
a wild obscenity at them, waving an ineffectual arm, then
turned and stamped away across the road.

Two hundred yards ahead, nearing the bottom of the hill,
the green Morris paused at the lights and the dark blue car
slowed, cruising in behind. A pale face crowned with fair
hair glanced back, without interest, and then the Morris
turned left, accelerated wheezingly into the side street.

The man in the passenger seat fingered the scar on his
nose thoughtfully. 'Is that it?' he asked.

'That's it,' said the man behind the wheel and drove
straight ahead, down towards the river and along Rabbit
Banks until he reached the Sunderland Road.

In a little while it began to rain again.

2

The offices of the Department of Health and Social Security
at Longbenton had the reputation of a prison factory.
Among the Newcastle people who needed to drive past its
security-conscious gates there was an air of desperation as
the afternoon drew to a close, because the vast numbers of
civil servants who emerged hurriedly from the dark-fronted
buildings would block the roadways for almost an hour. The
surroundings were bleak, the offices soulless, the size of
the whole building intimidating. Yet it was, Eric Ward
considered with a wry smile, the place where caring people
worked, where support was given to the needy, and the
unemployed, and the hopeless.

It was not a building he cared to visit, but it was con-
venient enough to call in there after his visit to the forensic
laboratories in Gosforth, where he had been consulting an
acquaintance of his in the police force about matters of
evidence that had been bothering him in a case he was
currently dealing with. He was, inevitably, kept waiting by

an imperious official at the gatehouse who demanded to know his business at Longbenton.

'Mr Hawthorne? Ah yes, one moment, please, while I check.'

He checked, and seemed vaguely displeased that Eric was telling the truth and was expected by Mr Hawthorne. He gave Eric unnecessary and somewhat inaccurate directions and told him where to park. His Cerberus role completed, he stepped back importantly into his glass cage, uniform buttons glinting in the weak sunshine.

Eric parked his car carefully. It was only recently that he had started to drive again, and he was still uncertain about driving any great distances. Since the operation on his eyes he had been in no great discomfort, but he was due for another check-up with the specialist in a day or so and was reluctant to take too many risks until then. So he used the car only for short-distance work in and around the city: his returns to Sedleigh Hall were accomplished by taxi, unless Anne was available to pick him up, when she was attending board meetings in Newcastle.

He entered the forbidding hallway, took the lift to the third floor and walked along the rabbit warren of corridors until he reached the offices used by Nick Hawthorne and his staff. The girl at the desk smiled brightly, recognizing him, and told him he was expected so could go straight in.

There were two men in the meagrely furnished office.

Nick Hawthorne, rising to his feet behind his desk, was unlike the typical idea of the natty-suited civil servant. He was six feet two inches in height, shaggy-haired and awkward. His brown suit was baggy at the knees and hung uncomfortably on his massive frame as though it wished it were still in the department store and safe from ill-use and tea stains. His hands were massive, fingers marked with nicotine, but his brown eyes were friendly and his spreading, coarse features were warmed by his smile as he welcomed Eric and introduced the other man in the room.

'Eric, this is Jack Fraser. He works for OFT.'

The Office of Fair Trading, Eric translated automatically in his mind, still not used to the penchant civil servants seemed to have for speaking in capital letters. He smiled at Fraser, shook hands. The man was nearer to the civil servant image: like Eric, above medium height; slim, young, with an eager mouth and careful eyes, the sort of combination that would serve him well in his career, where a certain commitment was required, but blended with a capacity to avoid mistakes. 'He's been advising me on the possibilities in the Sam Turriff business,' Nick Hawthorne explained.

Fraser sat down, and Eric followed suit. Nick Hawthorne tilted back in his own chair and drew heavy eyebrows together as he nodded towards Eric. 'Mr Ward here, he's been acting for the Department in the prosecution of Turriff, but he's already told me the evidence is a bit thin. Now you say, Fraser . . .'

'You know this man Turriff, then?' Fraser asked.

Eric nodded. He knew Sam Turriff. He'd been around Tyneside grubbing a living for years. At one time, when Eric was still in the police force, Turriff had been known to have a hand in small-time prostitution in the Scotswood area. When the council moved in and dragged down most of the houses to replace them with neater terraces Turriff had turned his attention elsewhere, taking a slice of the one-arm-bandit boom in the working men's clubs in Durham. It hadn't lasted long as an enterprise because some of the London mob had moved north, set up local operations that squeezed out the small men, and then moved back south with local thugs installed. Turriff had drifted lower. A big, sack-shaped man with a meaty face and confident air, he had dropped out of sight for a few years and it was only recently, now that Eric was in practice as a solicitor on his own account, that he had re-emerged into Eric's professional life.

'I know him,' Eric replied, 'and his business. Personal loans arranged; anything from £10 to £100 without security.

And I've advised Mr Hawthorne that the Department can't touch him at the moment: not without harder evidence of wrongdoing.'

Hawthorne grunted and caressed his lower lip with a gentle finger and thumb. He shook his head. 'It just beats me, Fraser, how the hell the OFT came to license him in the first instance.'

Fraser's mouth developed a primness that made Eric think of elderly ladies twitching curtains at their neighbours. 'I don't think you appreciate the OFT's position,' Fraser said. 'You'll recall the legislation of 1974 demanded consultation over licensing between local authority trading standard officers and the OFT—'

'And it was scrapped to save money,' Hawthorne growled.

'It became . . . negated,' Fraser amended to his satisfaction. 'It meant that when Turriff put in his application for a licence we didn't know about Turriff's criminal background, nor that three years ago he was prosecuted for a number of offences contravening the terms of his precious licence.'

'If the OFT had troubled to *ask*,' Hawthorne said bitterly, 'we could have told you that his charges regularly amount to an equivalent annual rate of interest well into four figures. The OFT was set up partly to stop that kind of abuse. Damn it, there's been one case where the rate worked out at 6,742 per cent!'

'Mr Hawthorne, you really must understand! I could talk to you about staff shortages, flaws in the Consumer Credit Act itself, erosion of our powers by a government committed to saving money. I could add also that there's been an explosion in the growth of moneylending and public demand for credit and loans. But the fact is, almost anyone with £80, an address and a postage stamp can become a licensed moneylender!'

'It's crazy!' Hawthorne expostulated.

'You don't need reputable referees, a proven financial track record, or even evidence of your own credit-worthiness,' Fraser emphasized. 'The Act doesn't even demand a clean police record. Just two simple forms and an application fee and you're in.'

'And you're happy with that state of affairs?'

'Of course not!' Eric listened as the edge of missionary zeal that had been lacking in Fraser's defensive tones now crept back, unbidden, but sharpened by Hawthorne's implied criticism. 'Look, we've got twenty staff in London to vet the fitness of about 16,000 applicants for licences which cover banking, insurance broking, debt collection and credit reference agencies. Licence demands are rising rapidly. There's no way we can do the job. And the system—'

'What system!' Hawthorne scoffed.

'A hamstrung system, but that's not the fault of the OFT people! Look, we vet the applicants, but our powers are limited! We have no right to search police records to check previous convictions. That's one.' He flicked up one elegant finger. 'We have no right to check bank accounts or other personal financial information. Two. Three: we have no right to notification of prosecutions by police or by the DHSS. And four . . .' He paused, flicking up a fourth finger dramatically. 'There is, as you know, no automatic liaison with trading standards officers, those local officers with whom we're jointly responsible for enforcing the licensing law. We didn't even *know* Turriff has already had convictions. How could we be expected to know, when processing 16,000 applications?'

There was a discreet tap on the door; it opened and the young girl from the outer office peered in nervously. She explained that the tea trolley had arrived and could she bring in three cups? She could, it was decided, and the charged atmosphere grew less tense as the plump, middle-aged woman in the white coat bustled in with the tea. Hawthorne peered gloomily into his cup as though expecting the worst; his mouth twisted as his expectations were confirmed. He sipped discontentedly at the tea, and then set the cup aside. He shrugged.

'All right, so we've heard your problems, Fraser. Now, you'd better hear mine.'

It was not new to Eric. Since he had accepted a few cases from Hawthorne he had heard the argument several times. The region was stumbling into critical depression: the whole of the North-East was dying still. The mines had gone, the shipyards had followed. There were 500 young unemployed for every job vacancy. Young men believed they would never find work; middle-aged redundant workers were resigned to the scrapheap. And social security benefits were not enough to live on.

'It's all very well,' Hawthorne was insisting indignantly, 'for successive Chancellors of the Exchequer to lift their noble brows and contemplate what is to be done about the oversubsidized unemployed. The fact is, there are no jobs and the money isn't enough. It's against this background that men like Sam Turriff have crawled out of the woodwork. Whatever his past life was like, he's sitting pretty now— he's got a bloody house in Gosforth, among lawyers and bankers!'

'I understand that, but—'

'Understand, hell! *I* don't! The moneylenders are a curse. Their interest rates are catastrophically high, but there are few poor households that can resist the temptation of a fistful of ready money—however cruel the economic wheel they're strapping themselves to! They're being desperately exploited, but when the ticket-men come to the door, offer ready cash without the security a bank would demand, they grab at it. They borrow £100 and pay back £150. And that's just the start. When they really get grabbed they'll end up paying thousands to make men like Turriff fat—or they'll end up broken in the Tyne. I want it stopped, dammit, I want it stopped!'

'There is a provision under the Act—'

Eric leaned forward and shook his head. 'The safeguard against extortion doesn't work, Mr Fraser,' he said quietly. 'I know these people who borrow have the right to challenge the terms of the loans through the county courts—but they won't do it. It's foreign to their background: they abhor involvement with the law, because to them the law is suspect. It also means that they'll never get support from a money-lender again; they'll be blacklisted; worse, they may get beaten, robbed, burgled. It's a vicious spiral, and they can't get out of it.'

Fraser was silent for a short while and then, stiffly, he said, 'I feel as though the OFT is on trial here. That's not fair. Now we've been furnished with the facts we can take action. We shall now inform this Mr Turriff that we intend to take his licence away.'

He did not add what Eric already knew, that the procedure was complex and lengthy, that there were no provisions for suspension or the imposition of temporary restrictions, and it could well be that it would be a year or more before Turriff could be called upon to cease trading. And even that was not inevitable.

After Mr Fraser had left them, slightly huffed, and with the militant zeal in his eyes still burning but now overlaid with the hurt of criticism, Nick Hawthorne leaned back in his chair and looked at Eric. 'I know what you're going to say.'

Eric smiled. 'The man can't help it. He's stuck in an impossible position.'

'Like all those poor bastards north and south of the Tyne who've got hooked by Turriff and his ilk. Eric, I'd love to nail Turriff, make an example of the sod, maybe put a shiver among the rest of them, slow them down a bit.'

'They'd argue they provide a social service.'

Hawthorne managed a grin after a moment. 'Aye, they're thick-skinned bastards and can turn an argument. And in a sense they've got the protection of their clients, who can't raise ready cash any other way.' He paused, gloomy again, and contemplated his littered desk. 'But you'll be giving me bad news.'

'You know it already. I've been over the papers. You've

not got enough to catch Turriff with. Harder evidence; someone to talk—that's what we need.'

'Evidence . . . like what?'

Eric thought for a moment. 'One of the abuses the OFT was intended to combat was the illegal possession of welfare payments as security against loans.'

Hawthorne grunted. 'Aye, I know about that. Turriff claims he'll lend cash without security, but I've heard well enough that his ticket-men insist on taking welfare payment books as security.'

'That,' Eric said, 'is a criminal offence. And so is the direct soliciting of custom.'

Hawthorne nodded. 'I'm aware of that. But evidence— *hard* evidence—of that kind isn't easy to come by.'

'Without it Turriff will stay unmolested as a loan shark.'

Hawthorne was silent for a little while. Eric waited. He knew what doubts would be churning in the official's mind. There was only one way to get the evidence they required, but it meant breaking the rules of the game as far as Hawthorne was concerned. The DHSS man had done all he could: Eric was sure that Hawthorne would have done his utmost to persuade individuals to utter truths, issue complaints, but had been unsuccessful. But it would go against the grain to ask an outsider—even a solicitor—for help.

'You know what you're asking me to do,' Hawthorne said at last in a doubtful, growling tone.

'I'm not asking you to do anything.'

'You want me to break confidences. You want me to open up confidential files.'

'We *both* want Turriff brought to book,' Eric said quietly.

'I don't know,' Hawthorne replied uncertainly, but he rose and walked across the room to stand beside the grey steel filing cabinet. He pulled out the top drawer, riffled vaguely through a number of files, clucking his tongue anxiously. 'I don't know,' he repeated, but when he came back to his desk he was carrying several manila folders. He placed them, unopened, in front of him and stared at them. He shook his head. 'Do you know any of Turriff's runners?'

'I used to know a number of his *associates* in the old days, but I guess this business he's into now is rather more specialized—and rather smaller beef as far as his henchmen are concerned. They'll be little men.'

'Sprung out of all kinds of rotten Scotswood woodwork,' Hawthorne agreed mournfully. 'There's one or two swum into our reckoning. I could give you a couple of names.'

'They're unlikely to respond to anything I might ask,' Eric said, 'unless there's some other kind of trouble hanging over them.'

Hawthorne opened his eyes wide and stared at Eric in mock protest. 'Do I detect suggestions of blackmail in that remark?'

Eric grinned. 'Friendly warnings never come amiss.'

'Mmmm.' Hawthorne hesitated. 'Don't suppose you've got anything on a character called Ferdy Newton?'

The name meant nothing to Eric. He shook his head. 'Is he one of Turriff's ticket-men?'

'He is. He works the Gateshead bank, it seems. I've come across him once or twice. Evil little character. But not helpful. Now if you could get something on him . . .'

'I could put some people on to it,' Eric said. 'But it still skirts around the real problem.'

Hawthorne eyed him unhappily. He put out a hand and gingerly touched the manila folder on top of the small pile. 'You want names.'

'There's no other way. It's unlikely I'll get anything tough enough on this man Newton to make him shop Sam Turriff. After all, quite a few villains have got their feet wet in the Tyne when they've grassed on their comrades. No, I need names of people who might be persuaded to testify against Turriff, or Newton, or whoever. They don't even need to make a statement, or put in a court appearance. All they have to be prepared to do is tell us whether they've actually handed over a welfare book. After that, I'll do the rest.'

Hawthorne shook his head. 'It means opening up confidential files,' he said again, 'and I don't like doing that.'

'All I need is a few names.'

Hawthorne sighed, and nodded. But he did not open the manila folders. Instead, he just said, 'There's a family in Byker: husband, pregnant wife, two small children. Name of Corey. The flats along the Sunderland Road in Gateshead —there's an unemployed steelworker called Lawson. An ex-Shotton man called Carter was employed for a while in the Leisure Department, he's badly down on his luck, got a drink problem.' Hawthorne glowered gloomily. 'They've all got some sort of problem, or are inadequate, or feckless, or have a criminal record. Some of them have just had bad luck, like Tony Cullen, but the names I've given you, they're people who certainly have one thing in common. Or maybe two.'

'Yes?'

'The one thing is they're all getting pretty desperate; near the end of their tether. One or two of them might turn to crime, do a bit of burglary. But they're all on the damned edge of a precipice, and they have that in common.'

'The second thing they all have?'

'Turriff,' Hawthorne said shortly.

'They've all borrowed money from him?'

'In varying amounts,' Hawthorne said. 'And my guess is they're having one hell of a job trying to pay back the loans. You might try them: if we could only get any one of them to bring an action for extortion . . .'

'Can you let me have the addresses?'

Hawthorne put his head back, stared at the ceiling and slowly gave the addresses to Eric. When they were all written down he looked at Eric sharply. 'You'll interview them?'

Eric hesitated, then shook his head. 'Not necessarily. I'll make some . . . inquiries first. There's a man I know, a character who's well-known and trusted on Tyneside. It may be he could make the approach better than I. But I'll see what can be done.' He rose, extended his hand to

Hawthorne. 'With a bit of luck we'll get Turriff where even the OFT can nail him, hard.'

'I hope so.' Hawthorne shook hands, and saw Eric to the door. Before opening it, he paused and glanced back towards his desk. 'Let's be clear,' he said.

'Yes?'

'I didn't open my files to you.'

'No, Mr Hawthorne, you didn't open your files.'

3

Every house in the tightly packed terraces of the west side of the city seemed to own at least one mongrel guard dog. Jackie Parton had seen them cringing up and down the steep streets of Old Benwell and Scotswood during the day in ragged packs; the price of pet food to keep them alive was a necessary cost to their owners, as was the price of low-cost insurance, mortice locks and household alarms. The crime rate in the West End was still rising steeply, petty burglaries and muggings heading the list. The dogs could keep an intruder from the door at night.

The assignment Eric Ward had given was hardly a productive one. Jackie Parton was well-known along the banks of the Tyne and beyond: he had been a successful and popular local jockey who had made the Newcastle Races his own stamping ground. Injury, the northern mobs, the suspicion of bribery and a bad beating had ended his career but his reputation was still sound among the pubs and clubs from Scotswood to Walker Gate. And people were usually ready to talk to him.

But not now, not about the loan sharks. He had known, vaguely, the first man Eric had mentioned to him, and felt able to question him directly. The reply had been direct.

'I'm unemployed, man, and I got a hundred-pound loan, yeh. It's The Debt, you knaa? I get my dole each week, and

I hand over twenty-five quid to the ticket-man. You don't need to know who he is. The Debt's to buy things for the kids. I canna go to the bank; and the wife's got her Catalogue, she buys things on credit from it and we pay back in bits, two quid a week for clothes and that. And then there's the house: door's been kicked in twice in a month. I know the lad who done it, but he's a big massive feller. I tell you, wor Jackie, I wouldn't try to stop him if he broke in . . . So don't talk to me about loan sharks, man, I got enough troubles already, you knaa?'

He got a similar story along Arthur's Hill and beyond the river bend in Byker, below the towering shadow of the Wall. They needed the money; they knew they were paying extortionate rates of interest; they were aware that Sam Turriff and others like him were getting fat and rich. But where was their choice?

It was a depressing business, and hopeless. He told Eric so when he met him outside the Nelson Street Job Centre in central Newcastle.

'They're caught in a trap, Mr Ward, even if it is partly of their own making. They're redundant, unemployed, got responsibilities and outgoings they see as commitments. They're taking their dole money but it's not enough, and in a little while they lose their pride too, and go to the likes of Turriff. Once hooked, they see no escape route. If they go to court, they can get the rate cut down, aye, but doors close to them. And they got an inborn distrust of the law anyway. Lawyers isn't for working folk.'

A steady crowd of people, mainly young men, a few with punk haircuts but others dressed in a standard uniform of sweatshirt and jeans, was passing through the Job Centre. Things had changed in the last twenty years, Eric thought: the old Labour Exchanges had been dour, uninviting build-ings with a stale, hostile atmosphere. The new Job Centres had fresh lighting, bright cheerful colours inside and young receptionists who looked as though they cared. The general appearance was closer to an art gallery than a place where the desperate might come to look for work, but the display was a series of cards, pitifully few in number, that announced the day's total of available jobs. A rough count would suggest some four hundred. A considerable number of them were located in the South and South-West.

'Geordies think two miles away from their Mam is two miles too far,' Jackie Parton said, almost reading Eric's thoughts.

Eric nodded. 'Local jobs are few and far between.'

'Rare as a raised lavatory seat in a nunnery,' Parton agreed.

'And just the climate for a loan shark like Turriff. So, you've had no success so far. How many names have you got left?'

'Just one. Tony Cullen. He lives up in a high rise flat in Stepney, near Byker Bank. I can make the call this afternoon, Mr Ward.'

Eric hesitated, glancing at his watch. He had arranged to meet Anne back at their own flat in Gosforth at six, there was nothing pressing back at the office except for his appointment with a man called Heckles at four-thirty, and he was curious to discover just what problem was facing Jackie Parton. 'I think I'll come along with you, Jackie.'

'Fine with me, Mr Ward.'

The little ex-jockey had parked his car in a side street. He ambled along on his bowed legs, chattering to Eric as they made their way across Grey Street, once described as the finest street in Europe, and down past High Bridge until they neared the old Assize Courts. Jackie had parked boldly but illegally; he had also been fortunate in that no traffic warden had marked his car. It was possible it was known, and deliberately ignored: the ex-jockey had acquaintances everywhere. Eric waited while the little man manoeuvred the battered Ford out of its tight space, then got in beside him as they followed the one-way system past the sheer drop of Tyne Bank and the sixteenth-century cottages that still clung to its sides. They turned north again and then drove

along City Road towards the high rise area near Byker
Bank.

The blocks of flats reared starkly out of the dreary streets
that surrounded them. They had been painted in colours
that had once been described as gay: now those colours had
taken on the drabness of their surroundings and had peeled
irregularly, while the concrete itself had blackened and
weathered badly. Eric knew the interiors would be as badly
maintained: the high rise areas generated little pride of
ownership; they had become refuges for the desperate.

Jackie parked the car and locked it in a litter-scattered
yard in front of the block. Uneasily, he eyed some youngsters
playing a desultory game of handball against the line of
brick garages, then he shrugged. 'Nothing they can cop in
my bloody car, anyway.'

He led Eric into the block of flats. The lift, predictably,
was out of order. The graffiti on the walls of the staircase
were amusing, crude and equally predictable in their sexual
messages.

Tony Cullen lived on the seventh floor.

He answered the doorbell after a short wait. He was about
thirty-five years old, of medium height, with tight, curly
hair and a freckled face. His light blue eyes were friendly,
if overshadowed now by a doubt his surroundings would
have fostered. His face should have been rounder and probably would have been, but something had thinned his
cheeks, pared down his jawline, the razor of experience
slimming away some of his good looks. He had shaved, but
carelessly, and there was a shadowed blue on his upper lip.
He wore a hand-knitted sweater of some antiquity, and blue
jeans with casual shoes. There was a certain wariness in his
tone as he asked them who they were and what they wanted.
It was clear that strangers in the flats were not normally
received with open arms.

'I'm Jackie Parton, and this is Mr Ward. He's a solicitor.'

Something happened to Tony Cullen's mouth. Its edges

hardened, stubbornness setting its line. He looked directly at Eric, and the doubt left his eyes. He knew all about lawyers.

'I'd like to have a talk with you,' Eric said reassuringly. 'About your circumstances . . . but nothing official. We're merely seeking some information. And maybe we're here to offer some help.'

'This . . . this about Kate?'

Jackie Parton glanced at Eric quickly, and then shook his head. 'Kate your wife?'

'Daughter,' Cullen corrected him. Some of the doubt crept back into his eyes. 'If it's not about her . . .' He hesitated for a moment, eyeing them both, then he shrugged. 'You better come inside.'

He led the way along a short passageway, past a closed bedroom door, and into a cramped sitting-room. The furniture it contained was elderly but well cared for; the room itself was tidy, if lacking the touches that a woman might bring. Eric gained the impression that the room itself displayed a dogged, independent pride; an insistence by its occupier that he could look after himself. And perhaps after Kate, too.

'So what is it you want?' Cullen asked, leaning against the window-frame with his back to the river slopes and his arms folded across his chest.

Jackie Parton hesitated, glanced at Eric. 'It's about Sam Turriff.'

There was a short silence. 'What about him?' Cullen asked warily.

'We understand you've borrowed money from him.'

The arms tightened across Cullen's chest, and an edge of truculence entered his tone. 'Now, wait a minute. If you're from Turriff himself, or from that little bastard Ferdy Newton, you can back off. I slipped a few payments, sure, but I'm up to date again now and there's no screws you can put on me, so—'

'No, Mr Cullen, you've got it wrong,' Eric intervened.

'We're not here on Turriff's behalf. We're trying to do something about him, and his kind.'

Cullen stared at him uncomprehendingly. 'I don't get this. *Do* something about him?'

'He breaks the law. He uses extortionate rates. He's a loan shark who trades illegally and the DHSS want to nail him. I'm acting for the DHSS at the moment, trying to get information.'

'Such as?'

'Whether he—or his ticket-men—are using direct approaches to possible clients. Whether he takes "security" from his clients by demanding their welfare books, signed in advance, and holds them against repayment of the cash due to him.'

'So who told you I was into Turriff for money?'

The silence grew around them as neither Eric nor the ex-jockey explained. At last Cullen moved away from the window and sat down in a lumpy easy chair. He did not invite his visitors to take a seat. He glared at them and anger seeped into his voice. 'The bloody DHSS officers . . . My affairs are my own, confidential. If they pick up any information, they're supposed to keep it to themselves, you know that? *You* know it, you're a bloody lawyer! But someone up there at Longbenton's been talking, about things they don't even know about!'

There was a vague prickling at the back of Eric Ward's eyeballs, the first signs of tension, a reminder he resented of glaucoma, and pain, and limited vision. 'Mr Cullen, we're just trying to help.'

'Oh aye, I'm aware of that,' Cullen said bitterly. 'But what kind of help is it, when the bloke you're trying to help ends up worse off than before? You just don't know what it's like, man, you and the rest of your bloody kind! You're all so quick to talk about laws and rights and all that, and you can spout about it when you're in court, but once the rest of us, the ones you're supposed to be helping, are out of the front door you couldn't give a damn. Except to chase

us for your bloody fees! Help? You're only out to help
yourself in the long run!'

Eric gained the impression the man was talking about
something other than Sam Turriff; his bitterness was
directed towards other, more tangible contacts with the
legal profession. 'All we want is some information,' he said.
'There's no real reason for you to be involved—'

'I don't intend to be!'

'But if you can merely tell us what methods Turriff or his
ticket-man has used—'

'And then you'd haul me into court to give evidence, isn't
that it?' When Eric hesitated, Cullen said triumphantly, 'Go
on, tell us! My talking here means damn-all, you'd still want
us in court to testify!'

'Mr Cullen—'

'Oh, howway, man!' Cullen said in disgust. 'Haven't I
told you I'm not going to be involved? Look, the fact is I
got a life to live. It's not easy. I got no job, though I look
every day, chase everything I can since I was laid off at
Swan Hunter's. I got no great lifestyle, but *I* built it and I
don't owe anything to anyone—except a bit to the ticket-
man as the bloody DHSS have told you. But that's because
I got a bairn. She's a bonny lass, and I'm not going to see
her short. But it's *my* business and no one else's. *I'll* look
after her, and I'll not have anyone else nosing in to interfere.'

There were undercurrents of dogged antagonism in his
words that Eric could not identify or explain. Jackie Parton,
familiar with the fierce pride that northern men could develop and responsive to that independence that thrust
through Cullen's outburst, shuffled uneasily, aware that
they were on shaky ground. Eric too felt edgy, knowing he
was losing control, unable to get through to Cullen, make
him understand there was no real threat in what he was
trying to do. 'It's not our intention to interfere—'

'Intention's worth nothing. I'll not have my behaviour or
my needs or my way of dealing with my problems called
into question.'

'So you won't help us, over Turriff or his ticket-men?'

'I got nothing to say.'

There was a short, awkward silence. Cullen sat staring at his shoes, sprawled awkwardly in his chair, resentment scarring his mouth, seemingly delving into levels of disillusionment and anger that had nothing to do with Eric and his companion. Only after several silent seconds had passed did he drag himself back to their presence. He looked up at them, his brows dark. 'You got anything else to ask?'

'Not if you can't help us on Turriff.'

'Then you better go. Kate'll be back soon, anyway. I don't want you here when she comes in.'

There was a photograph on the sideboard. The child looked about five years old. The field was sunny and she was smiling. She wore a print dress. 'Is this your daughter?' Eric asked.

'You'd better go.'

It was clear that Cullen held deeply possessive feelings towards his daughter, even to the extent of not wishing to discuss her with strangers. Possessiveness mixed with fierce pride in her, for that had come through also. An odd combination, in Eric's experience. A man with pride in his daughter was usually only too happy to talk about her.

At the door, a certain change came over Cullen. He relaxed somewhat, seemed to lose some of the aggressiveness that had overtaken him in the sitting-room. He seemed uneasy, a little upset. 'Hey . . . Mr Ward.'

'Yes?'

'I . . . I'm sorry for that, back there. I mean . . . well, I got a bit annoyed, because I got to thinking about other things, nothing to do with you. There was no call for that. You're doing your job.' The doubts were back in his eyes again, as he glanced towards Jackie Parton and back to Eric. 'Fact is, I've had my problems, and it's no joke bringing up a kid without a mother, you know? As for Turriff, well, you're right in a way to go chasing after him, but there's fifty Turriffs on Tyneside, and if you get in a tight spot there's no one else to turn to. You understand?'

'I understand.'

'I'd like to help, but . . .'

His eyes drifted past Eric across the city. Across the river, in Salt Meadows, the towers of the power station were dark against the skyline, but Cullen's glance seemed to be searching beyond, to the haze above the Durham hills, blue in the distance. Perhaps he was looking back rather than into the future; or maybe he was unseeing, looking inwards for something that was lost, or irrecoverable, like yesterday's confidence.

He was still standing in the doorway when Eric and Jackie Parton made their way along the barriered landing and down the stairs to the car park.

Someone had deflated one of the car tyres. No one was now playing handball against the garage walls.

4

Eric got back to the Quayside at four-thirty in the afternoon. He parked on the quayside itself, in the shadow of a Norwegian freighter moored in the river, and walked the short distance to the Victorian building that had served the mercantile community for a century but which now held his office, among others. He was the only lawyer in the tall stone building: companies drifted in and out of the premises, some staying only a matter of weeks.

It was hardly the centre of business activity in Newcastle, tucked away at the foot of the bank, but it suited Eric: he enjoyed the ringing stone of the old, sweeping stairway, the high-ceilinged rooms, the splendour of the oak banisters. From the narrow window of his office he could see the quiet quayside and imagine its ancient bustle where the Tyne uncoiled its slow curve to the sea. He could still see freighters, cutters, corvettes nosing their way along its dark waters, and naval vessels and foreign hulls still frequented the quay, but what he enjoyed was the atmosphere of the place, the Victorian dignity, stolid and secure, that gave him a feeling of belonging, even if it must deny him from time to time the kind of lucrative contracts other, better situated solicitors enjoyed.

He accepted the kind of business he wanted to accept.

The Heckles affair was something else: he had doubts about it. Now, as he returned to the Quayside and asked at reception whether Heckles had arrived, he felt a certain sense of relief that he had not.

'Has he phoned in?'

'No, Mr Ward.'

'No message otherwise?'

'None.'

Eric went up the stairs to his office and dealt with a few outstanding files. Half an hour passed and there was no sign of Heckles. He rang down to reception, knowing they would be leaving the office soon. 'If Heckles does call in the next ten minutes, okay, I'll see him. After that, before you go, if he rings in then fix an appointment for early Tuesday.'

He did not ring in.

Eric had felt a certain sense of relief at the non-appearance of his client, but it was overlaid with a sense of guilt. He tried to explain it to Anne, when they sat down that evening to a quick dinner at the Gosforth flat. She had done some whirlwind shopping at Eldon Square: she sipped a good Médoc now, and shook her head.

'I just don't see why you feel guilty. Any more than I understand why you have to take on such doubtful cases.'

'It all came about somewhat accidentally. And,' he added somewhat shamefacedly, 'I suppose it was also due to the fact I've never liked Mason much.'

'Mason?'

'Detective-Superintendent Mason. I've known him quite a while. There was a period when we were on the beat in the city. He always was a bully and his methods were crude. They were based on putting in the boot first, asking questions later. His phrase was "getting in his retaliation first".'

'Charming.'

'It raised trouble unnecessarily. All right, we went into some tough areas, and the city centre on a Saturday night was never a picnic, even when the dogs went in. But Mason seemed to attract problems, if you know what I mean. His methods were well known and people reacted badly to his methods.'

'Unlike your smooth approach.'

'You're laughing at me,' Eric said severely.

Anne grinned. 'Not really. But this Mason character— what's the connection with your client Heckles?'

'I just happened to be in the Crown Court when Heckles was remanded. The lad had no legal representation. Mason was demanding police custody, opposing bail. It seemed . . . the youngster needed help.'

'So you offered your services?'

'Something like that.'

'A youngster, you said?'

'Well, in his twenties, you know.'

'I *do* know. *I'm* in my twenties! Youngster, indeed!' She pulled a face at him, and it was Eric's turn to smile.

'Youngster or not, according to your lights, I got him out of Mason's clutches.'

'It *was* a drug charge,' Anne said doubtfully.

'Suspicion of illegal possession,' Eric corrected. 'And certainly not proven.'

'Even so, you don't see yourself as a criminal lawyer dealing with the gutter life of Tyneside. At least, *I* don't see you in that light. You know well enough there's a job to be done with Morcomb Estates, and it would more than fill your time. As it is, I've had to engage Mark Fenham now, and though he's well enough qualified, and bright—'

'And has good connections,' Eric said, grinning. 'Come on, you know well enough young Fenham can do a far better job than I can; a first class lawyer, and a landed background!'

'*Young* Fenham is my age,' Anne said crisply.

It was good enough; it had sidetracked her from the battle she was always eager to wage with him, the insistence that he should work for the company her father Lord Morcomb had left her. It was not what Eric wanted: he valued his independence. More; he needed it.

'Young as he is, Heckles is younger, and with none of Mark Fenham's advantages. I don't know very much about his background, and he's certainly been addicted, but my guess is he's kicked the habit now. Unfortunately, his name's still on police books, and when Mason's keen to get a quick resolution to a case he can be somewhat precipitate in his judgments.'

'All right, and you've shown him up, with the case against this Heckles man dropped for lack of evidence. But I see no need for you to pursue the issues any further.'

It was difficult for Eric to explain it to himself. He had spent long enough on the beat during his years with the police force to see the thuggery that could incur in the West End, to appreciate the squalor that many lived in and to understand how crime could spread like a cancer through whole families and generations. Understanding was one thing; condonation was another. The step from fighting crime, from running in thugs with knives and bricks, from uncovering city corruption, to *creating* evidence to put people away had been too large for him. But there were men on the Force, like Mason, who had never been above that kind of activity. It would have happened, possibly, with Heckles, had Eric not taken his defence, won him bail. And now that the charges had been dropped, in some obscure way Eric felt his involvement should not yet cease. He was not keen to tarnish the image of the police for he had been one of them; but perhaps because he *had* been one of them he felt it necessary to make sure that men like Mason did not get away with doubtful practices.

'So, although Heckles didn't turn up this afternoon, I don't think I can let it drop. I'll have to try to get to see him, explain things to him, try to get him to take action. I'll probably have to go to him, rather than have him come to my office, though. These people just don't trust lawyers—'

'And I'm beginning to have the same feeling myself,' Anne said. She sipped her wine, her eyes smiling at him over the rim of the glass. 'Among *others*. Do you know I haven't seen you for three days . . . and nights?'

'If you will go to London on business . . .'

'I thought maybe we could have had a leisurely morning tomorrow, relax like we used to, and then drive to Sedleigh Hall—'

'After I've seen Heckles.'

Anne sighed theatrically. 'You know, I'm beginning to think you were right. You're too old for me.'

'Tell me that later.'

'You'll just go to sleep.'

'Don't count on it.'

Some hours later, as a shaft of moonlight picked out the patterns in the duvet that lay crumpled about them, Anne stirred, flung an arm heavy with lassitude across his chest and whispered, 'Do you *really* need to chase this Heckles thing tomorrow?'

'I think so.'

She sighed. He felt her breast warm against his arm. He half turned towards her. 'It shouldn't take long.'

'Make sure it doesn't. I'd like to get away north early as possible. You haven't forgotten the shooting party?'

Eric hadn't forgotten. It was something he had not been looking forward to, but he had not forgotten it.

In a little while, Anne slept. Eric remained awake, considering the contrasts in his life: this flat, Sedleigh Hall, and shooting parties on the moors; a drug addict, a loan shark, and an appointment in the morning he hadn't told Anne about.

*

The room was small, but dark and cool. The ophthalmic surgeon sat facing Eric, his right knee lightly touching Eric's left as the light probed deep into the eye. It was a curious sensation and one Eric had still not come to terms with: it was as though he were floating in a sea of darkness with one, isolated point of light lancing into his skull. It was unreal and it was draining of thought and feeling.

'It's been quite useful,' the surgeon said chattily, 'this recent trend for opticians to record intra-ocular pressures as a matter of course, when they fit people up for glasses. Of course, like other physiological data, intra-ocular pressure varies over a wide range . . .' He switched off the light and adjusted his position to probe the left eye. 'You driving now?'

'Recently started.'

'Not going too far?'

'Just local.'

'You getting much halo effect at night?'

'A certain amount.'

'Hmmm. Can't be much, though . . . The rainbow halo, you see, arises because the fluid droplets and corneal œdema, produced by raised intra-ocular pressure, produce a diffraction effect. The light gets broken up into spectral colours.'

'Interesting,' Eric said drily.

'Yes. Headaches still occurring?'

'Much reduced.'

'Nocturnal vomiting?'

'Not at all.'

The light snapped off, and the surgeon slid his chair back, rose and went across to his desk. The diffused, restful light soothed Eric's nerves as the surgeon made some notes, his back to his patient, and then he turned and smiled. 'Simple peripheral iridectomy can cure acute closure glaucoma for ever, Mr Ward.'

'So I've been led to believe.'

'That assumes it's treated in time, of course. Most people who have severe ocular pain and blurred vision hightail it to the nearest doctor and get it treated. The more stubborn don't. You were . . . stubborn, I believe.'

It had been a time of pressure; a refusal to recognize a physiological weakness. Eric made no reply.

'However,' the surgeon went on cheerfully, 'I don't say the condition in your case wasn't caught in time. Drainage operations, iridectomy . . . did you know that trabeculectomy has proved itself to be the best operation in the English-speaking world?'

'I didn't.'

'The point I'm making is, you seem to be OK. Whatever traumas you may have suffered seem to be over. You'll still get occasional discomfort, particularly at times of tension; there'll be the odd headache and so on, but most of the symptoms you'll have suffered in the past shouldn't recur. There are, naturally, some prices to be paid for your . . . reluctance to face the issues in the first place.'

'Prices?'

The surgeon cleared his throat. 'One of them is obvious enough. In chronic glaucoma there's a cupped optic disc and a varying degree of visual field loss—an enlarged blind spot, arcuate scotoma above and below the point of fixation, gradually getting worse to give rise to tunnel vision. You've been spared most of that, now, as a result of the iridectomy. But you've had acute closure glaucoma and in such condition visual acuity can be quickly and seriously impaired —even down to 6/60. I've checked your visual field: it's impaired, as we'd expect. But not seriously, of course. It simply means your angle of vision is limited.'

'I was aware of that,' Eric said quietly. 'You mentioned more than one price.'

'Yes.' The surgeon paused for a moment. 'Restriction of the visual fields is physiological. The other price that I've observed—without any clinical testing, I hasten to add—is psychological.'

'How do you mean?'

The surgeon fluttered his hands vaguely. 'Well, let's put it like this. The blind—the truly blind—they come to terms with reality: they accept their condition, attune to it, develop a combative attitude towards it. Those who have faced blindness and who have been pulled back from the brink of that condition—people like you—sometimes seem to react in a different way.'

'What kind of reaction?' Eric asked.

'Life has suddenly changed for them in a manner difficult to define. Pain, sickness, blindness, an acceptance of a fate . . . and suddenly they can see again, properly, somewhat impaired perhaps. It's then that, psychologically, they never accept absolutes again. Not just physical absolutes— whether something is hard or soft—but emotional or personal absolutes—friends, enemies, lovers. They seem reluctant to accept reality any more. No . . .' He paused, thoughtfully. 'No, that's not it. It's not that they don't *accept* reality . . . rather, their sense of reality is blurred. Yes, that's right.' He smiled, aware of the apposite nature of the phrase. 'That's it. A blurred reality.'

It was a remark that drifted muddily in Eric's mind as he drove across Newcastle that morning on his way to the address where Phil Heckles lived. The surgeon had been indulging himself, of course; the only information he should have given Eric was the clinical summary, that the glaucoma was arrested, and that there should be a return to normality as far as his eyesight was concerned, other that the inevitable, irreversible, limited field of vision. The psychological comments had been mere speculation, not backed by research. Yet they scratched away at Eric's mind to score lines of doubt about his own reaction to life as it was now: his attitude to Anne and Morcomb Estates; his stubborn insistence on a Quayside practice; even his need now to go talk to Philip Heckles.

When he found the address it was not unlike the area in

which he had found Tony Cullen on the north shore, though that was perhaps to be expected. The car park was littered, pieces of rusting iron lying half-concealed in long grass at the edge of the park. Weeds grew dankly between brick garages whose doors hung crazily, broken from their hinges. The tower blocks on the skyline rose starkly above a wasteland of Victorian terraces that proclaimed their time and their heroes: Baden-Powell, Kitchener, Hartington and Northbourne.

It was among the double-fronted houses of one of those streets, commemorating a Radical who had not been above making bombs from metal as well as from words, that Eric found the client he was seeking. No. 5 Jacob Holyoake Street was a decayed Victorian building with a tiny, weed-infested front garden. Designed as a late-century terraced 'villa', it had faced the demands of the twentieth century by submitting to conversion into flats, but the ground-floor windows gaped starkly, the basement flat had been ripped open to the elements by vandals and the first floor was heading towards the same state of decrepitude.

The landing was dark, littered and pungent. Eric hammered on the door. There was a long silence.

'Heckles? Phil Heckles?'

There was no reply. Eric hammered again. 'This is Eric Ward. The solicitor. I was with you in court.'

There was the sound of reluctant movement behind the door. Eric waited while the shuffling movements came nearer; finally the door opened. Phil Heckles peered out, recognized Eric and turned away, leaving the door ajar.

Eric entered, followed the man into a littered, grubbily-furnished room. The curtains that hung at the window were ancient and dirty. The arms of the single deep chair were black with ancient grease. There was a stale smell in the air, food and unwashed bodies. There was no heating, and the room was cold. Somewhere he could hear a tapping sound, a broken curtain rod against a window-frame.

Phil Heckles stood listlessly, facing Eric. He was dressed

in a thin sweater, ragged jeans and the trainers on his feet were worn and stained. His body was thin as winter, and his face had a blue coffin look, eyes deep set as though retreating from the realities they perceived. His skin was drawn over sharp cheekbones, fragile, paper-thin, and he seemed to display an edgy indifference to Eric's presence in his room and in his life.

'I expected you at the office yesterday.'

Heckles made a slight shrug and looked at the worn carpet.

'You didn't turn up, so I thought it best I came to see you, to try to explain what I would have explained had you come to the Quayside.' Eric paused, but there was no response from Heckles. 'Look, you got arrested by the police. You were held for three days. You were questioned. You had a rough time. You were hauled up before the court for a remand in custody.'

'Yeh.' Heckles almost whispered the word.

'If you had been so remanded, I believe pressure would have been applied—real pressure. I know the man in charge: he would have got a conviction.'

Heckles looked up, something flaring yellowly in his eyes for a moment. Indifference returned.

'I got you off,' Eric went on, 'got you out on your own recognizances. And now the possession charge has been dropped. In other words, Detective-Superintendent Mason was aiming for an easy conviction, and with your record he could have got it. Given time. But once you were on the street again, it was too difficult.'

'I know all this, Mr Ward.'

'So now I'm trying to advise you. Tell you it's possible to take action in retaliation. Against the police.'

'I got a record.'

'You've also got rights. You can charge Mason with false arrest, assault, battery—'

'Now hold on!' Heckles raised a weary, warning hand. His fingers were heavily stained with nicotine. Eric had heard of addicts who, once they were off heroin, took to heavy smoking but would use only half a cigarette, allowing the rest to burn down to the fingers, oblivious of the pain. They would shrug off that pain as they shrugged off the rest of life: a mute acceptance of situations they did not want to discuss. Heckles was like that: a doomed, hopeless man of twenty-five, hair neatly cut for his court appearance, but hollow-eyed, nervous and quick in gesture, and depressed in spirit.

'You just want to leave it, then?' Eric asked. 'You don't want to bring charges—'

'Mr Ward, do you know about me?' Heckles asked, with a surge of bitterness in his voice. 'Look, six years ago I got attracted to work on the rigs. It was a rough life, but we lived it up . . . Amsterdam, rock, Paris . . . But when I came back three years ago I had five thousand quid in my pocket, couple of ounces of heroin, and the habit. Everyone I knew on Tyneside was into smack, dikes, morphine. It was a real scene, man! But of course, I got nailed.'

'Heckles—'

'Fines in the end took most of my cash, that what I didn't spend on the street. I was living in Byker. Friend of mine kicked down the door, threatened me with an axe, took my TV and sold it. It was wild . . . In the end I was broke, and I got registered only because I was sick of scoring in the street. Police hassling you . . . would-be gangsters trying to rip you off. But nothing changes. You get registered, and *doctors* rip you off. And the police don't change. Once they know you, they're ready to nail you. For anything.'

'That's why I think you should bring charges against Mason.'

Heckles shook his head. His hair was greasy and flecked with dandruff. The fire that had burned briefly in his eyes had died and he stared at his hands. Slowly, almost mechanically he rolled up one sleeve. 'See this, Mr Ward?'

Where the surface veins had once been visible along the inside of his arm there were now long, continuous lines of scar tissue, extending from the crook of his elbow to his wrists. When he turned over his hands their backs were in the same state. He shrugged. 'Tracks. Most junkies have them but I got worse because I shot Diconal.'

Eric knew what he meant. The chalk in the substance clogged the veins; inevitably, the veins collapsed, in time. There seemed little he could say. He stood in front of the young man and waited. There would still be days when Heckles would come alive, course with energy again, maybe even return to some of the wildness he had known as a youth on the rigs. But there was only one way in which that would happen: if he took a dose of heroin again. And even then the effect would be short-lived.

It was as though the thought itself suddenly penetrated Heckles's woolly mind. The dullness of his glance was lost; there was a bitterness in his eyes as he looked up at Eric. 'I'm off the skag. I get methadone twice a week. There's pills, and linctus to keep me goin'. But there's no pleasure in it, you knaa? I used to get methadone injections, but with the veins gone . . .' His narrow mouth twisted, displaying discoloured teeth. 'And it's I'm the guy who gets the pain. There's other cats, they got it made. There's bastards out there on the streets with big cars, flashy houses, money to burn. No one knows them, or admits to it. The coppers is punk, they'll do nothin' or maybe they're getting paid to do nothin'. But at least they could stop the dealers, the bloody middlemen who make sure the stuff hits the streets. They're the bastards I'd like to take!'

He grinned, wolfishly. 'One of these days I'll do it. If some bastard like Mason doesn't fix me up first. There's ways to skin cats, and when I pull a job it isn't going to be riskin' just a possession kick. When I go, I'll go in style, believe it.'

His mood changed again, chameleon-like. He bared his stained teeth to Eric, looking up at him wickedly. 'You ever hear that junkie joke?'

'Phil—'

'No, you ever hear it, Mr Ward? They say, you go for the
needle, you inject, and in the end there'll be just one vein
left. You know what they call that vein?'

'No.'

'They call it Custer's Vein.' Heckles cackled to himself
at the macabre joke. 'You get it? Custer's Vein. Inject that
one, and you've had your last stand . . .'

Eric was glad to get back out into the street. There was a
light drizzle in the air and he turned up his collar as he
made his way back towards his car.

He wondered briefly what the old demagogue Jacob
Holyoake would have made of the society he had so passion-
ately set out to make free in the nineteenth century. But
then he thrust away thoughts of Holyoake and Heckles from
his mind: the one man was long since dead, and the other
would hardly have long ahead of him.

There was nothing Eric Ward could do about either.

His steps echoed in the street, but he was hardly aware
of other steps, hardly aware of the man who had slipped out
of the doorway across the street behind him. The man
walked in parallel, making for the same destination. It was
only when Eric reached his car and began to unlock it that
he realized he had been followed. There were some quick,
short steps and Eric turned, looked around.

The steps slowed, the man stopped and Eric stared at
him questioningly. The man simply stood there for several
seconds, glaring at Eric aggressively.

Eric hesitated. 'You want something?'

The man made no reply, but just stared.

He was perhaps forty years of age. His bulky body was
clothed in a shabby blue suit. He had a heavy, red face with
a questing, curved nose in which wide nostrils quivered
suspiciously. His pinhead eyes were cold with malice; he
had mutton fists which clenched and unclenched in a display
of nervous anger that was somehow stained with anxiety.
His stance was aggressive and stiff, edgy as a spitting cat

ready to strike or flee. His thinning sandy hair seemed to bristle as he stood glaring at Eric, shorter by perhaps six inches and aware of his lack of height as Eric faced him.

'Yes?'

'I know about you.' The words struggled out painfully as though the man was short of breath, unable to force out what he wanted to say.

'You do?'

'Solicitor. Ward.'

'That's right.'

'What you been to see Phil about?'

There was a short silence. Eric turned back to his car. The demand crackled angrily from the man again. 'I asked you a question! What you got to do with Phil Heckles?'

Eric turned back, warily. 'I think that's my business and his. It certainly isn't yours.'

'Phil Heckles isn't any of *your* business. But then, that's your bloody problem, isn't it, *Mister* Ward! You keep going around sticking your long nose into all sort of affairs that got nothing to do with you.'

There was a short silence. Eric stared at the angry man. Calmly he said, 'There's clearly something you want to get off your chest.'

'Damn right there is. I'm telling you, friend. In the old days when you were in the fuzz, maybe you rated some protection. Uniform to hide behind. But those days is gone. All you got now to protect you is good sense. And you're not showing too much of that, at present.'

'Get to the point.'

'Stop nosing around here, and stop nosing around me!'

'You?' Eric frowned. 'I don't even know who you are.'

'So why did you put Jackie Parton on to me, then? I'm telling you, it's a big mistake. You can't go around putting someone on Ferdy Newton and think you can get away scot free, my friend. I'm telling you, Ward, you're meddling in things that could see you down a sewer.'

'I imagine those surroundings would not be unknown to you,' Eric said coolly.

The other man almost danced with rage, but Eric noted that he came no closer. The anger was real and solid enough, but it was still tempered with caution. 'You listen to me, Ward! Your best bet is to find some business up north with that high lady of yours and stay out of the West End and stay away from the south shore. Life can be fat for you as a bloody lawyer if you stay with the business that pays. The business you're nosing into won't pay—not for *you* it won't, not unless you think a hammering in an alley is good payment.'

Eric stared at the man thoughtfully. Names stirred sluggishly in his mind, out of context, but now beginning to fit. Slowly, he said, 'You're one of Turriff's ticket-men. Ferdy Newton . . .'

'And someone you'd better not cross.' Newton hissed out the words and squeezed the muscles around his eyes, trying to inject menace into them. It was a failure: they remained quick and nervous, unresponsive to his theatre.

Eric shook his head contemptuously as he stared at Ferdy Newton. 'I knew Sam Turriff in the old days,' he said. 'I knew him when I was on the beat in the West End and he was trying to make his way along the river. He never rated with me, because he was always a *small* man, in his objectives, and in his methods. And he never did make it, not the way he wanted to. And now—'

'You listen to me—'

'And now he's descended to the loan shark game. Not much further to fall. But I hadn't realized he's started to use scum like you. Rubbish from the litter-bins of Walker.'

Ferdy Newton was shaking in his rage. His pinhead eyes glared apoplectically and he raised his clenched hands in an impotent surge of anger. '*Scum!* You call me that! I warn you, Ward, I got more friends on Tyneside than you realize, and when you mess with me you mess with—'

'Turriff?' Eric leaned against the car door and folded his

arms. Coldly he said, 'I don't rate Sam Turriff now, the way I didn't rate him in the old days. You won't scare me off by using his name, or any of the loan sharks along the river. You're small time, Newton; you feed off helpless people and if I can put you out of business I'll do it. And all the puffed-up prancing threats in the world won't stop me.'

The bulky little man's nostrils quivered in fury, but he was regaining control of himself as he remained some six feet away from Eric. He glanced about him with a quick, ferrety movement of his head, as though to be certain they were alone in the dingy street. Then he rubbed one meaty hand against his lips. 'All right, Ward, so you think you're too big to worry about little men like me, and about Sam. But don't make the mistake of underestimating us. You've got too uppity; you forget what life was really like, the days when you were on the beat. You've gone up in the world, become a bloody solicitor, got married to a piece with a mansion in the country, but you've lost touch too. Lost touch with Tyneside. You don't know any more what life is like down by the river. Don't mess about with me. Don't go chasing up people like Phil Heckles, and stay well away from me.'

'I'm not chasing Heckles, I'm trying to help him. What's that got to do with you?'

'Just leave him alone. And stay away from me. You don't know the muscle that's around to knock you flat. That's all I'm saying.'

'Newton—'

'You don't know nothing, man. You don't even see Tyneside the way it was. You can't see the way it is. So *back off!*'

The bulky little man turned away, walked back up the street and paused at the corner just to look back briefly at Eric before he disappeared. Eric got into his car and sat there for a little while, thinking. It hadn't taken Newton long to realize that Jackie Parton had been making inquiries about him and Sam Turriff. It could mean the word would now go out quickly from Turriff to the ticket-men—and to the punters. It would take very few screws to make helpless people in these back streets who had already been lent money by Turriff to keep their lips tightly closed. The chances of getting any information on Turriff's methods would now be slim.

Something else bothered Eric. Ferdy Newton was a little man in every way, but his belligerence had been unexpected. It was possibly coincidental that he had met Eric here in Jacob Holyoake Street; on the other hand he might have been following him. Either way, he knew Eric had visited the junkie called Phil Heckles, so he must be well placed as far as Tyneside rumour and information was concerned. There was something more, again. The man's anger had something greater than Eric's inquiries to fuel it; maybe he was more vulnerable in some sense than Eric realized.

But it was none of these considerations that kept Eric sitting quietly in the car. Ferdy Newton's words had not been the same as the surgeon's: they had been concerned with an understanding of Tyneside, a knowledge that he claimed had deserted Eric since his embarking upon a new career as a lawyer. Eric wondered whether he was right. The surgeon had spoken of a blurred reality. There were many ways of defining that phrase.

Maybe it could be linked to what Ferdy Newton had said.

Such thoughts were fanciful. Eric Ward started the car and eased away from the kerb to swing into the main road and make his way back the two miles to the Swing Bridge. Once back at the flat he would leave the car and Anne would then drive them north, to Sedleigh Hall, to a dinner party, and tomorrow to the shoot on the moors below the Cheviot. That was a reality far divorced from Tyneside, but he was part of both. Still part of the city he knew so well, in spite of his involvement with landed gentry and businessmen in the Northumberland social scene.

He was vaguely aware that the fierce insistence of the thought held something of the defensive in it.

5

As usual, Davinia took her time in leaving the school buildings. She was almost always late arriving, but this was her
last few months at the school and the teachers bothered her
little: they were aware of the contempt she felt for them with
their narrow, bitter lives. She was far superior to them, in
knowledge, in ability to enjoy herself, and in her understanding of human nature.

Especially men.

Money was the problem. Her father had been a drunken
Irish labourer who had fallen into the river and drowned
when she was only six years old: she barely remembered
him. Her mother was a slattern from Birmingham who
never ceased to bewail the fate that had brought her north
with her husband and left her high and dry on social security
for all these years, trapped in the high rise blocks, living
from day to day, and misused by a series of 'gentlemen
friends' who never stayed longer than a couple of months
and inevitably walked out owing money in the area.

She had one brother, six years older than she, but he'd
left home at sixteen and was working somewhere in the
south as a lorry-driver. Once she was sixteen Davinia would
be heading south too—not to look for her brother but to get
a slice of the richer life available in London. She couldn't
wait to get rid of Tyneside mud.

But meanwhile, there were things to learn, pleasures to
enjoy—and they required money. And recently it had become a problem.

It was the bloody coppers, of course: they were to blame.
As she dawdled her way out of the cloakroom, licking the
fresh lipstick she had just applied, she muttered to herself
almost automatically, 'All coppers is bastards!' She believed
it. If they just left things alone, she'd be all right.

The first time had been for free, but she'd learned better

than that. He'd been a lad from Hebburn; she'd met him on a Saturday afternoon at the bus station, and a week later he'd had her in Leazes Park. She'd still been thinking of romance then, but she was only thirteen, and she hadn't seen his dust thereafter. Then there was the soldier up on the Town Moor; then the Dutchman from the freighter. It was only when the character who lived in the next street approached her that the message got through. He was fifty if he was a day. She'd seen the way he looked at her, and on that wet, drizzling night he'd suggested she went up the lane with him behind the terraces.

God, she'd been green then! Half a quid!

But she'd got the message and he'd given it to her. They'd pay, the older men. And with the money, she could reach for real pleasures.

Trouble was, the bloody coppers. Saturday nights they were out with the dogs in the city centre; they could hustle underage drinkers out of the pubs; and the Panda cars were always nosing around Elswick and Cruddas Park.

They hadn't yet latched on to the school, though, she thought, and a scornful smile touched her mouth. She caught her swift reflection in the panelled glass of the door as she went through into the school yard and the smile widened in self-satisfaction. She knew more than the bloody coppers! They hadn't twigged there was at least three of them, running the game fifty yards from the school gates.

And she was one of the sharpest.

The street was disappointingly empty. There were three punters who had been with her, from time to time, during the last month, and she knew their cars. Not one of them was in sight, and Friday was usually a good day, money in pockets, tension eased before a night out with the lads.

They'd passed the word, of course. It was what she wanted them to do. Some of the big men, the older men, they liked young girls. She could handle that, though she despised them, their beery whistling breath, the horny-skinned hands, and the mindless thrusting. She could stare at the sky or the darkness and think of other things, the way it would be south in the clubs, the highs she could reach. So she *wanted* them to pass the word, so she could while away the months before she escaped south.

But the street was all but empty.

Davinia hesitated, dawdled at the school gates, holding the rough iron in one hand, pulling at it, swinging on it, watching the road. That stupid kid was standing there as always, little Miss Prim, eyes down, staring at her feet, waiting to be picked up.

But the only car in the street, parked, was one she'd seen before. Dark blue one. Her mouth twisted. It was the bastard who'd given her a rough time earlier in the week. It would be her turn this time, Davinia O'Hara's turn. She could walk up there, give them a mouthful, and she could be away before they could get out, lay a hand on her . . . She released her grip on the gate and began to walk purposefully towards the car.

As she walked, her temper cooled. All right, they'd given her a bad time, bruised wrist and knuckles to show for it. But they could still be punters. No reason for her to jump to conclusions. Maybe she hadn't made it obvious enough. Maybe they'd got the shivers, thinking there was a copper nearby and they got scared, shoved off before she could make it clear she was no scruffy amateur. She straightened, slowed her walk, put more swing into her stride and the secret, knowing smile came back to her lips.

She walked towards the dark blue car.

There were two men, again. They were the same characters who'd been there early in the week. One of them was vaguely familiar, apart from that earlier meeting. They were looking past her, ignoring her. She was fifteen feet from the vehicle when the engine started up.

She stopped. She wasn't getting caught a second time. The man in the passenger seat was staring at her now, and there was a blind tension in his face that frightened her.

The car began to edge forward, the engine tone rising, and Davinia made a decision. She stepped back, away from the kerb, pressing herself back against the low school wall. She wanted nothing to do with these men.

The man with the scarred nose gripped the edge of his seat, fingers curled in tension. The car swung out from the kerb, past the girl standing against the wall, and his eyes flicked past her, down towards the school gates.

They had timed it carefully. The driver had said, moments ago, 'Clear now. We've got maybe two minutes. Let's do it cleanly.'

It would be clean. There could be no trouble, no opposition, no muscle to fear.

The car nosed down the road, dipping into the slope, nearing the school gates. The girl standing there, somewhat forlorn, still had her hands laced together, her head down. She seemed hardly aware of the approach of the car.

The man with the scarred nose gripped the door-handle. The car slowed, came to a stop just six feet from the school gates. The door opened. The girl looked up.

She could not have known, could not have expected it. Even so, some intuition electrified her, made her eyes widen in sudden panic, made her drop the purse she was carrying. Her mind told her to run, the tension held her rigid, unmoving, and the man with the scarred nose stepped from the car, strode swiftly towards her, and only then did she turn to run back into the school yard.

He caught her before she had gone five yards. His fingers clamped on one arm, she was yanked to a stop and then his powerful hands swept her up, cradling her roughly as she kicked in wild terror and at last found her voice. She screamed, once, as she struggled, but the man was turning, dragging open the door of the car, bundling her inside.

Someone shouted above them on the hill. In the rear mirror the driver caught sight of an overalled man waving an arm, ineffectually. Down the hill, to their right as the car pulled away, tyres screeching, a middle-aged couple looked about them vaguely, hardly aware of what was happening. In the passenger seat the man with the scarred nose gripped the girl tightly. She was trembling, but made no sound. Her slim body was rigid, her eyes wide and staring. The driver was sweating. He tried to say something, but his mouth was dry and the car picked up speed, roaring down the hill, gears crashing as he made a clumsy change with a shaking left hand.

The lights ahead of them were red. Waiting there was a battered green Morris. It held a woman and two children.

The blue car swung right into a side street, fifty yards from the lights. By the time the lights had changed, and the green Morris began to cough its way into the steep slope of the hill, the blue car had disappeared.

Outside the school gates there was an overalled man, talking earnestly with a puzzled, middle-aged couple. When the green Morris stopped they stared at it hesitantly until the woman got out, spoke to them. After a short, increasingly agitated discussion, the woman got back into the car and reversed into the school gates, crunching a bumper against the wall, and then clattered her way down the hill.

Fifty yards above the gates Davinia turned away. They hadn't been punters, after all. Either way, it was none of her business.

CHAPTER 2

1

The spectacular thunderstorm that had provided the backdrop to their conversation the previous evening, during dinner, was over. The deep cracking sound of thunder and the brilliant flashes of light that had edged the hills against the blue-black sky had now given way to high birdsong and bright morning sunshine above the fell. There was a light breeze from the north-east and it brought a hint of salt with it though they were miles from the sea. The Land-Rovers were a mile below them huddled together like grey and blue beetles at the foot of the track; ahead of him Eric could see the marching lines of conifers swathing the northern rises with heavy, solid green, but to his left the moors rolled, dipping and rising, crossed by boggy streams, grey-green and open, and perfect shooting country.

The first of the hunters was already making his way back. Eric was surprised to see it was Liam Geraghty. Of the eight-strong party, which comprised, apart from himself, Anne, Mark Fenham the young solicitor, Geraghty, Lord Finborne, Dennison, Paul Morris and John Helstone, the last person Eric would have expected to return early was Geraghty. He had a greedy eye, for business and for anything else, and it seemed uncharacteristic for him to make his way back towards Eric, sitting alone on the grey crag, observing proceedings. Equally surprisingly, Geraghty came alone: his financial adviser Dennison, who had barely left his shoulder last night, was still some two hundred yards out on the moor.

Anne had chosen the shooting party with care. Eric had taken no part in the discussions she had held with young Fenham, letting them get their heads together on the planning of it without interference, but he noted with wry amusement the names of the people who had been discarded. The Lord Lieutenant, for instance: if it was to be largely social, the weekend would certainly include him. Lord Finborne's presence, of course, gave the occasion a certain appeal to the snobbish, but Finborne was no landed clod: he had spent a period in London in a merchant bank, held a considerable overseas portfolio, and was a member of the board of Anne's company, Morcomb Estates, Ltd. Paul Morris was an accountant with a large practice in Newcastle and a stake, through his mother's family, in a chain of food stores in the North-East; John Helstone was a banker of some presence and reputation who had been responsible for the far-sighted financing of the Newlink enterprise in Cumbria.

The shooting was incidental.

Eric had played little part in the conversation the previous evening. He knew Finborne fairly well, and Morris and Helstone slightly, but apart from desultory conversation with them he had maintained the discreetly polite role of host while Anne dominated the discussion, first with her warmth which on such occasions could light up the room, and secondly with her keenness of mind in the business discussions that followed dinner. He had, however, observed Liam Geraghty and his man Dennison. The financial adviser was sharp, a small, slight man with an accountant's eyes, probing remarks, peeling away defences, questioning comments instinctively. Yet for all his sharpness he seemed to shrink beside Geraghty.

It was not merely that Liam Geraghty had an awesome physical presence. He was well over six feet tall, weighed some sixteen stone, and had hands like hams. His voice was deep, silky on occasion but positive and determined when he wished to thrust home a point. His beefy features were marked by a high, ridged nose that jutted arrogantly from his face, but his eyes were narrow and watchful. Yet it was not the physical things that Eric recalled about him after last evening's first acquaintance. Rather it was the lust that flickered behind his dark eyes, the greed that touched his fleshy mouth in unguarded moments: the impression of a lust for power and a greed for success. Money he had already, in plenty: he had built up a successful dairy operation in Ireland years ago, had translated that success to a West Coast company in the States, and diversified into light engineering with a panache that had surprised even his friends. Not that he would have many, Eric guessed, unless he found them useful. He was a committed man with tunnel vision: his objective was clear—self-aggrandisement in business terms—but the rest of the world would remain unobserved. Perhaps even his personal life intruded but little. Eric wondered what kind of family life he had ever enjoyed in his clawing to the top of a business empire of international proportions.

'Had enough, Geraghty?'

The big man slowed at Eric's question, and glanced up to him, seated on the crag. His eyes were narrowed to slits against the glare of the sunlight, but he smiled. It gave his features a certain charm, the kind that could fool opponents.

'Well, I'll tell you,' he said, breathing heavily from the exertion of the climb up from the moor. 'They talk in Ireland about the Irish football referee who suggests the players should play extra time now, in case the weather gets bad later. I've never subscribed to that philosophy. I do something for as long as I find it enjoyable. Then I stop—whatever the weather. There's never a question of extra time.'

For Geraghty, enjoyable would mean profitable. Eric wondered vaguely what would be profitable in the Irish businessman's joining him on the crag.

Liam Geraghty laid down his shotgun, broken open, on the springy turf and sought a place to sit down near Eric. The breeze ruffled his greying, curly hair and he exuded self-satisfaction as he beamed around him, the businessman at play on the northern moors. 'Grand country,' he said. 'I can understand why you'd live out here. But you don't shoot, hey?'

'Hand guns. I've never taken much to the shotgun or rifle.'

'Hand guns,' Geraghty said thoughtfully. He squinted up to the blue, cloud-flecked sky. 'That would be something you learned when you were in the police.'

'That's right.'

'But not something you carried on with. No obsession.' Liam Geraghty paused for a moment, broodingly. 'Obsessions is bad things. They can take over your life completely. My father now: he had a youthful obsession that he could drink any man under the table. He became the traditional, jacket-off, stage Irishman in the end, ready to take on any comers. It killed him, of course . . .' His voice trailed away and silence fell. Then he shook himself, throwing off memories that had no place on a bright Northumberland moor, and he glanced towards Eric, grinning suddenly. 'You know what my old man said to me once, when I asked him why he drank so much? He said it whiled away the time until he got drunk.'

Eric smiled vaguely. He was still waiting to learn why Geraghty had sought out his company. 'They'll be following you in, soon.'

The desultory crackle of the gunfire had all but ceased now. Dennison had turned, was walking back towards them. Across to the left Morris, Helstone and Lord Finborne were breaking their guns, ready to turn back. On the right, Anne and Mark Fenham were standing together, the solicitor still firing.

'Well set-up young feller,' Geraghty observed.

'He is,' Eric replied, guessing what was coming. Geraghty would always be a man interested in seeking out chinks in armour.

'They seem to get on well together. Much of an age, they are.'

'He won't be a great deal older than Anne,' Eric agreed.

'They seemed to get their heads together a lot, last evening.'

'Fenham's employed by Morcomb Estates. He's a bright young lawyer. He'll make a name for himself. They'll have had business to discuss.'

Geraghty glanced at him, almost contemptuously. 'Why don't you do something about it?'

'About what?'

'I was divorced ten years ago. Kicked her out. Got back from Florida and caught her at it. Bloody Waterford man.'

'I've been divorced too,' Eric said coolly. 'It's not the prerogative of the Irish.'

'I didn't mean . . .' Geraghty scowled, hesitating. 'You're a cold fish, Ward.'

'I prefer to call it control.'

'Either way, you're a fool. This chap Fenham, he's good. He'll set himself up with a seat on the board of that company of hers. You should watch him—in the company and outside it.'

'I'll bear your suggestions in mind.'

'Like I said, you're a cold fish and a fool. The company doesn't need Fenham: you could do what he's doing easily enough. Probably better than he can. And a seat on the board is there for the taking. What holds you back? It can't be that scruffy practice of yours down on the Quayside.'

Eric was silent for a few seconds. Geraghty's tone held a certain impatience that seemed out of character. He was leading up to something, waiting for something, and it stained his tone, sharpened his conversation in a manner that puzzled Eric, as much as the man's returning early from the shoot puzzled him. He glanced sideways at the big Irishman. 'What do you know of my practice?'

Geraghty snorted. 'I know it isn't worth a damn! Let's be clear about something. If I go into a business deal I never go in with my eyes shut. I always get to know the other feller's strength and weakness. I thought in the case of Morcomb Estates you'd be one of the strengths. Turns out you're nothing. You're not even involved! Oh, inquiries on Tyneside tell me you got qualities that are often lacking in lawyers—guts, integrity, all that crap. But they also told me you're a fool. A rich wife, a big business, and you stay out of it.'

'It suits me.'

'To deal with small-time stuff, hippies and drunks, petty crime and the odd taxation job thrown in? I don't understand you, Ward.'

'I *thought* I understood you, Geraghty.'

'Eh?' The big Irishman's back suddenly stiffened and his head snapped around to stare directly at Eric. His eyes were hooded and his lips hard-edged. He spread thick fingers on the granite, gripping away the sudden tension that seemed to have arisen in him. '*Thought* you understood me? What's that supposed to mean?'

Eric hesitated, then shrugged slightly. 'Just as you've run a check on me and my business, so I've summed you up as much as I can in our short acquaintance. I'd heard about your business interests, of course, and formed some kind of opinion from them. And I watched, and listened to you, last night. It gave me a general picture.'

'And?'

'The picture is somewhat fuzzy this morning. Clouded by your behaviour.'

'What about my behaviour?' Geraghty asked harshly.

'It's out of character. You've walked over here, ahead of the rest. Now you're here, you seem unsettled, edgy. And you've gone out of your way to be boorish and unpleasant. Yet you've nothing to gain by that. I'm unimportant to you; I'm not involved in your business deals. And even if I were, it's unlikely I'd be affected by your boorishness into giving you the favourable terms you hope to get.'

Geraghty hardly seemed to be listening. Eyes narrowed, he scanned the moor, and yet he seemed to be taking nothing in. Tension still raised ridges in the back of his hands, and he glanced quickly at his watch. Then, as some of Eric's words sank in, he looked across again. 'You didn't say much last night.'

'No.'

'You let young Fenham talk. You didn't put your oar in.'

'But I could have.'

'On motives?'

'Something like that,' Eric said quietly.

Geraghty nodded, biting at his lips. 'I thought as much.' But he seemed unworried, nevertheless, about the prospect of Eric's intervention. The tension that lay within him was occasioned by something else, as he sat glaring out across the moor to where his financial adviser, Dennison, was striding back towards the crag.

*

The business conversation during the previous evening had largely involved Geraghty, Fenham, Anne and Lord Finborne. Finborne owned estates on the northern border, just south of Berwick, and extending inland in a swathe of moorland that enclosed several small villages. Morcomb Estates had grown since Lord Morcomb had died: within a small period of time Anne had expanded her landed interests, partly as a hedge against inflation, and partly to take advantage of tax concessions regarding forestry holdings. She had proved she was developing into an astute businesswoman, and though she still occasionally harped on about Eric's taking a more positive role in Morcomb Estates, they were both aware that her own business acumen was increasing to the extent that she needed no husband to lean on, lawyer or otherwise.

Geraghty's plans were vague, though positive enough in concept. He had set up several meetings to negotiate the purchase of land from Finborne and from Morcomb Estates, and these had culminated in the shooting weekend. The insistence that the weekend was necessary had been his: three weeks earlier he had phoned to suggest a meeting in Northumberland and Anne had agreed to arrange it. It would be an opportunity to get Geraghty over from Ireland and on her home ground.

They had not, nevertheless, been able to get much out of Geraghty with regard to his business plans. He talked vaguely of expanding fishing processes along the north Northumberland coast, largely as a tax device; he was interested in the mining potential in the southern slice of Finborne's holdings; he had discussed European funding possibilities for the development of rural areas, notably two of the villages that law athwart Finborne and Morcomb Estates land, and he had expressed an interest in purchasing one stretch that presently was open, untouched and unplanned for.

Mark Fenham was quite convinced what Geraghty's intentions were. At one point in the evening, as Eric had been checking that the supply of cognac was enough to see the evening through, he had caught part of the young lawyer's conversation with Anne. Geraghty had moved away to light an enormous cigar and had been buttonholed by Morris and Helstone, each with their own interests to pursue. Finborne had made his way to the cloakroom, and Anne and Mark Fenham were standing to one side as Eric came up to them. Fenham had looked about him conspiratorially. 'I've got it sussed out, Eric.'

'You have? Good. Your brandy glass is looking rather light.'

Anne shot him a furious glance, part annoyance, part mockery.

'Tax dodge,' Fenham said simply. 'I'll certainly take a little more brandy.'

'It'll be across in a moment,' Eric said and moved away. As he did so, he heard Fenham remark, 'Geraghty's on to the most recent swindle. He'll buy up the land, announce he wants to use it for agricultural purposes, draining the boggy area south of Beacon Crag, and then take advantage of the subsidy the Government will pay to *stop* him turning over the use. Which he'll never have intended doing anyway because of the prohibitive cost of the drainage. I'm convinced of it, Anne . . .'

It was a possibility, Eric had admitted to himself, but not a likely one. There were other reasons, and quite simple ones, for Geraghty's interest in Morcomb and Finborne holdings, but they would be rather more ambitious than the plans the young lawyer was so confident about.

But that still didn't explain Geraghty's behaviour this morning, on the sunny crag. And even in the weekend shoot itself, there was something odd, something Eric had not yet been able to puzzle out, but which lay disturbingly, fluttering at the back of his mind.

*

They were all gathering at the crag now, beaters, dogs, hunters. Finborne looked elegant and at ease with his broken gun over his right arm, leather-padded shoulders lean, slim-hipped, the measure of an English gentleman. Morris's lack of fitness was showing in dampened hair streaked across his brow and Helstone was breathing hard too, but well satisfied with his kill. He was known to have a keen eye with a gun as well as in business.

Anne came in last, with Mark Fenham. The young lawyer was casually dressed, and for the first time Eric looked at him with completely objective eyes, beside Anne. He was as tall as Eric, leaner, younger, and there was an enthusiasm about him Eric had not noticed before. The moors had stripped away his normal carefulness and he was relaxed. Anne was holding his arm almost possessively, and she was slightly flushed, warm and happy, with red-gold glints in her hair. Eric remembered seeing her like that once, right at the beginning, pacing down on her mount through the woods above Sedleigh Hall . . . He was suddenly aware of Liam Geraghty's eyes on him and he glanced at the Irishman. There was a sardonic smile on the big man's face. A sour edge of resentment suddenly slivered through Eric's veins.

He held Geraghty's glance for a moment, then said, 'Shall we go down?'

The Irishman smiled, then fell into step beside Eric as he turned towards the track. In desultory fashion the others began to follow, down to the Land-Rovers at the bottom of the fell, and a lunch of chicken and champagne.

Sandy soil crunched under Eric's boots. The resentment was still with him, compounded of dislike of the Irishman's boorishness and perhaps his own fears. 'This deal you're working at with Morcomb Estates. You've not said much about your plans if it goes through.'

Geraghty grunted as his heel turned on a stone and he almost stumbled. 'Damn . . . No, not said much, but that's because there's a lot of thinking to do about it.'

'Rubbish.'

Slowly the Irishman swung his heavy head to stare at Eric. Something moved deep in his narrow eyes, too deep and too vague to be recognized. 'What's that supposed to mean?'

'You've no intention of doing anything with the property you buy.'

'And why should you think that?'

'I *know* it. Just as you know there's no great business advantage in buying up the designated areas from Finborne and Morcomb Estates.'

Geraghty crunched along beside Eric silently for a short while. 'If I haven't told you what I intend doing with the land, how can you suggest there's no business advantage?'

'Because I know what other holdings you have, Geraghty.'

The Irishman almost stopped, then recovered himself. 'What holdings?'

'France and Germany. I read the financial press. Closely. And I'm familiar with your subsidiaries.'

Somewhere high above them a lark was singing; below, as the heat of the day began to increase, the distant Cheviot seemed to shimmer in a slow dance.

'You've been doing some odd homework for a man who won't play in his wife's company, Ward.'

'The fact I'm not involved doesn't mean I'm not *interested*, Geraghty.'

The big man was silent for a little while. The rest of the group had fallen some distance behind them as Geraghty asked cautiously, 'All right, so what's your deductions regarding my interest in Northumberland?'

'Your power base has moved from Ireland of recent years, even though you still retain the quaint Irish image for your products. Your company is now effectively, and certainly for tax purposes, US based.'

'So?'

'The USA has a tax treaty with the UK. American-based companies distributing profits from the UK subject to mainstream corporation tax will, in the next year or so, see the rate they pay fall from over forty per cent to around twenty-five per cent.'

Geraghty was breathing heavily. 'And that's a good reason to buy land in Northumberland?'

'It is if you buy cheap, do nothing with the land, but value it highly in your returns. The US operates a worldwide tax credit system. It means that US subsidiaries can *average* income from a low tax country, such as the UK is now becoming, with income from high tax countries—like France and Germany. You *need* the land in Northumberland to take advantage of disappearing tax allowances and roll your tax liabilities forward until they become taxable at future lower rates. You could have done better with an investment in manufacturing industry in Britain, or high technology companies, but maybe that's in your plans too. At the moment, land in the north will do for a start. Buy cheaply, value highly in your returns.'

The lark song had faded, and the silence of the moors had returned. Geraghty clumped along beside Eric, saying nothing, but his head was up, his arrogant nose questing, almost sniffing at the wind. 'It's a theory,' he said at last. 'But only that. I . . . I gather you haven't confided in your wife.'

'I haven't.'

'This kind of . . . theory, it could cause her to raise her price.'

'It could.'

'So why haven't you told her?'

'I haven't been asked.'

Geraghty's smile was twisted. 'Still staying out of her business affairs, is that it? Or is it something different? Maybe you just want to show her that her legal adviser, the young and handsome Mark Fenham, is just a snotty-nosed kid when it comes to big business, hey?'

The resentment was sour in Eric's throat now. He held it in check. He had brought this on himself, in his attempt to

score over Geraghty for the man's ill-humour and boorishness. If he descended now to the Irishman's level, he was
lost. In more ways than one, for it could create sores that
might not heal.

'No, nothing like that, Geraghty. I simply wanted to know
whether I was right—and I think I am, in view of
your reaction. And there was something else I wanted to
know.'

'Is that right?'

'It's something that's been puzzling me. About last night.
About today. About the whole weekend. I'm just surprised
that you—'

'*What's that?*'

Below them the track levelled out to the open, flat area
flanked with gorse where the Land-Rovers were parked. To
the right the land dropped into a steep gully crossed by a
small wooden bridge which drove the track into a belt of
trees, silver birch and alder. Ferns grew on the slope in
profusion and on the far side of the slope the track dipped
among heather-clad hills. Along the track a Land-Rover
swung its way. On its roof a blue light flashed.

'Police,' Eric said in surprise.

'What do they want up here?' Geraghty's voice was thick,
edgy with a sudden tension and his breathing seemed constrained. He quickened his step as the police vehicle bounced
and lurched over the tussocky grass towards the parked cars
of Eric's party. It came to a stop and the passenger door
opened. A police officer stepped out, in the familiar black
and white peaked cap. He raised a hand.

'Mr Geraghty?'

Liam Geraghty stopped. Eric glanced at him; the Irishman seemed to be shaking slightly as he stared down the
hillside to the questioning policeman. At last he raised his
own hand. 'That's me. I'm Liam Geraghty.'

'Do you think we could have a word, sir?'

The big man hesitated for a moment, looked quickly at
Eric and then hurried down the slope. Eric made no attempt

to follow him; instead, he waited until Anne and Fenham joined him.

'What's happening?' Anne asked.

'I don't know.'

Geraghty had reached the police Land-Rover. The policeman was leaning forward, one hand on Geraghty's arm, talking earnestly. The Irishman stiffened, his arm jerking away from the restraining hand suddenly, and the policeman stepped back, motioning towards the door of the vehicle. Geraghty almost blundered forward, dropping his shotgun, and clambered into the police car.

Eric glanced swiftly at Anne and then began to move down the slope. The Land-Rover's engine roared, the vehicle was thrust into reverse and then straightened, swung in a sharp arc to head back down the hillside.

'Mr Geraghty!' It was the financial adviser, Dennison. He seemed anxious, nervous at being left alone with the shooting party. He was hurrying down the hillside, pushing past Eric, but he was already too late. Whatever it was that had drawn Geraghty into the police car, it was important enough for him to lose all interest in his companions on the moor. As the Land-Rover accelerated towards the bridge he cast no glance backwards.

His departure left Dennison disconsolate, making public the businessman's indifference towards his financial adviser. The man's voice drifted shrilly. 'Mr Geraghty . . .'

The thin, reedy tone was lost on the spreading, sunlit hillside. The thunder of the Land-Rover's engine faded towards the distant road to Newcastle. In a little while the birdsong returned to the fell.

2

It was several days before the news broke about Liam Geraghty. For Eric it had been an uneventful few days. He and Anne had been surprised and concerned at the abrupt departure of the Irish businessman, and the shooting party had inevitably discussed it, though not at great length. Dennison had not stayed: he had taken his leave immediately they returned to Sedleigh Hall. His departure loosened tongues a little but there was an odd reluctance to spend much time in discussing Geraghty. It was as though embarrassment at the appearance of the police on the moor had stifled normal reactions.

In the privacy of their bedroom, Anne was less inhibited. Eric was not sure whether the mystery of the Irishman's departure had spiced Anne's weekend, or whether she was somewhat piqued by the occurrence. What *was* certain was that she was intrigued.

'What on *earth* do you think it could have been about?' she asked as she snuggled into Eric.

'I've really no idea.'

'You don't suppose it'll be anything to do with the IRA, do you?'

'The IRA?' Eric unwound his arm from about her shoulders and laughed. 'That's a bit fanciful.'

'Well, he *is* a sort of expatriate Irishman, isn't he, living in the States much of the time, and many of those people tend to be pretty hot about the old country and that sort of thing, and maybe he's been gun-running, or something.'

'I doubt it.'

'Well, maybe he was arrested for something else.'

'What makes you consider arrest?' Eric asked.

'You don't get dragged off a moorland shooting party for nothing,' Anne said, sniffing. 'I mean, it must be for something serious. I think he's been arrested for some nefarious business deal or other.'

Eric made no reply. He wondered whether she was closer to the truth than she realized. Geraghty was a ruthless businessman; he would have sailed close to the legal wind on more than one occasion.

'Anyway, it's extremely rude,' she insisted, 'dashing off like that.'

'Dashing off so *mysteriously*, you mean.'

'Same thing.'

At the beginning of the week Eric was in the Crown Court with Eldon Samuels, a young barrister who displayed ability and a loose tongue: the latter would probably, in time, restrict the flowering of the former. But he was a useful source of information and gossip. Eric took coffee with him at the interval for the adjournment, making no attempt to raise the incident on the fell, but wondering at the same time what Samuels might have heard about the matter.

It seemed he had not. Instead, he was bubbling about a different matter entirely.

'It'll be breaking in the newspapers tomorrow, maybe this evening, you mark my words! Unless the police try to put a muzzle on it, of course, and I can quite understand if they do.'

'How do you mean?'

'An immense cock-up, of course! I mean, there are occasions when the boys in blue really do make fools of themselves. *You* know as much about that as any, Ward: you were one of them. Don't tell me you never heard of cover-ups, or restrictions upon embarrassing stories.'

'So what's this one about?'

Eldon Samuels had a thin, pinched face and reddish curly hair which seemed reluctant to crawl up his skull: he was prematurely balding. He also had the habit of tugging at his sideburns when he was enjoying himself, as though he thought the action might stimulate the growth. He tugged now, enthusiastically. 'Well, it seems it was all set up. You'll know there's been concern for some time about the use being made of provincial airports for the drug traffic in the North. Less crowded, less sophisticated in surveillance, the northern air terminals have been a better bet for the smugglers than Heathrow.'

'I'd heard.'

'Well, there's been no crackdown at Teesside—small

terminal, bit isolated, easy place to seal off if you really
wanted to nail the boards down. But nothing's been done
because, *I'm told*, the police have been gearing themselves
up to a strike against the dealers. They've had an informer
for some time, working in Newcastle and Sunderland, and
it was only a matter of waiting for the shipment to come in
so they could pounce and take not only the shippers but
also the dealers.'

'And?'

'It only just blew up in their faces, didn't it?'

'How?' Eric asked, a trifle impatient at Samuels's stretch-
ing out the tale.

'*Well*, it seems the nark had told the boys in blue about
the safe house. Chester-le-Street, of all places. Down behind
the church there. Anyway, they didn't dare put any surveillance on the place . . . no point anyway, since it was clean
until the Teesside shipment came in with the courier. So,
they played it cool, waited until the shipment came in, noted
the courier, saw him head up the A1 and congratulated
themselves. All they had to do was wait until the dealers
showed up, and then the cat could pounce.' Samuels smiled,
tugged at his reddish sideburns again. 'Trouble is, didn't
happen that way.'

'What did happen?'

'Unbelievable, really, unless you know our friends in blue!
First of all, a tanker overturned on the A1 and the lads
trailing the courier got delayed. Delayed, mind you, for a
traffic accident! Then, inconceivably, the back-up didn't
arrive before the courier did, wasn't sure whether the man
had gone into the safe house or not, wandered down the
road towards the traffic accident . . . I tell you, it makes
you wonder . . .'

'The outcome, I imagine, is that they didn't catch the
dealers,' Eric said drily.

'Nor the courier, dear boy! He'd wandered away after
dropping the stuff, to mind his own business, very sensibly.
But more than that, when our friends the fuzz finally arrived

at the Chester-le-Street house they were even too late to deal with the next bit of nefarious activity.'

'What was that?'

Samuels grinned: his teeth were yellowish, one of them chipped at the front. 'This is the enjoyable bit. *Someone* had confounded everyone. Not only was the courier gone and the dealer not arrived, but the *package* was gone too! While everyone was doing their Keystone bit on the side of the goodies, and the baddies hadn't woken up to what was happening and were still doing their nervous, walk-sideways bit, some character nipped into the safe house, lifted the material and shot off, rapid as they say.'

'And the police—'

'Have no idea who did it. So, they have nothing on the courier, can't nail the dealers, everyone's accusing everyone else, and there's a chunk of heroin swilling around Tyneside *uncontrolled*. I mean, it's cheap enough at the moment with the dealers selling at just five quid a packet, but when this skag hits the streets, with the purveyor keen to make a quick profit and out before the heavies get to him, the kids will be high on *pennies*.'

Samuels drained his coffee and set down the cup. He picked up his brief papers and nodded towards the door. 'They'll be back in soon; better make a move. Thing is, you know, whenever I get one of your erstwhile colleagues on the stand I admire their stolid, perfect commitment to duty and consider they do a grand job. Am I impressionable? Must be. Because when I learn of a cock-up like this one, I begin to worry about the efficiency of British justice. Or the police arm, at least. Mustn't knock our own contribution, hey, Ward?'

He winked and began to make his way towards the door. 'Grab the papers tonight, anyway. See how they try to cover up this story. The editors will never let them bury it, believe me.'

But in the event, they were never forced to face the embarrassment. The headlines, and Press attention, were taken up by a bigger, human interest story. One that explained why Liam Geraghty had hurried away from the fell on Saturday morning.

Anne met Eric in the drawing-room at Sedleigh Hall when he arrived home from the Crown Court. She held a copy of the evening paper. Silently she handed it to him. The headline was splashed heavily across the front page: GERAGHTY HEIRESS KIDNAPPED.

'Had you heard about it?' Anne asked breathlessly.

Eric shook his head. 'I came straight from court, and didn't stop to pick up a paper.'

'It's been on the six o'clock news. But it happened last *Friday*, Eric! Why on earth have they waited until now to break the news? That poor Mr Geraghty!'

Poor. Hardly the word to apply to Liam Geraghty, the Irish tycoon. Guiltily, Eric thrust aside the thought as unworthy. 'They'll have held the news back maybe to deal with the kidnappers, maybe to try to stop them before they realized the whistle was blown. I don't know. Anyway, let me read the account . . . and I can do with a drink.'

'It's been a hard day?'

'It has. So I'll settle for whisky for once.'

Eric sat down and re-read the headlines.

A police spokesman today broke the news that the grand-daughter of Liam Geraghty, the well-known Irish businessman, was kidnapped from Newcastle last Friday. The exact circumstances of the kidnapping are still undisclosed and some mystery also surrounds the reason why the thirteen-year-old girl was living in Newcastle, but the delay in announcing the crime remains equally unexplained.

To date no contact with the kidnappers has been made by the police and Mr Geraghty was unavailable for comment. It is understood that Mr Geraghty was informed of the kidnapping on Saturday morning and since then has been in constant touch with the police.

Liam Geraghty holds extensive dairy produce interests in Ireland but of recent years has extended his business to take up holdings in America, France and Germany. He was divorced from his wife ten years ago and has one daughter, Ruth, who is the the mother of the kidnapped child.

'Whisky . . . and a dash of dry,' Anne said, interrupting his reading. 'I've kept the hard stuff in short supply.'

'Thanks. It's been a rough day. Stuffy court, and stuffier judge. And Eldon Samuels.'

Anne grimaced and sat down, perching herself on the arm of his easy chair. She was wearing a light perfume: he caught a trace of it as she leaned back and gestured towards the newspaper he was holding. 'Funny business, entirely. I mean, not for the things that are said, but for what's *not* said.'

'I haven't finished it yet,' Eric replied.

It is understood that Ruth Geraghty is now living in the United States, but attempts to contact her for comment have failed. The police spokesman was unable to confirm that Mr Geraghty has arranged for his daughter to fly to Newcastle.

Liam Geraghty was in England when the kidnapping took place. Our sources inform us that he was entering into certain business transactions with Morcomb Estates, Ltd and was being entertained at the home of Mrs Anne Ward when the kidnapping of his granddaughter took place.

'Fame at last,' Eric murmured, and tossed the paper on one side as he sipped the whisky Anne had poured for him. He grimaced. He had cut out alcohol apart from the occasional drink; when he took it now he was always vaguely surprised that he bothered. He had largely lost the taste for it, and yet it seemed the appropriate thing to reach for when he was tired, and tense at the end of the day.

'So what do you think?' Anne asked, slipping her arm across his shoulders. Eric glanced up to her and shook his head.

'Don't you think it's odd?' she insisted.

'There are some . . . curiosities about the account.'

'Tell me.'

Eric glanced at the newspaper again. 'In the first instance it's a rather *constrained* account. It's not been sensationalized in the way one would normally expect. It's not often we get a kidnapping on Tyneside—and certainly not the grand-daughter of an Irish tycoon. I would have expected them to have made more of it.'

'I was thinking of rather more practical things.'

Eric smiled. 'All right, you be the advocate.'

She slid forward slightly so that her hip was pressing against him. 'Well,' she began in a self-satisfied tone, 'you may see nothing odd in it but have you noticed that the account speaks of Ruth Geraghty?'

'Presumably that's her name.'

'But not her *married* name!'

'Maybe she's not married.'

'She's got a daughter!' Anne said indignantly.

'And *we* slept together before we were married.' Eric grinned at her. 'Has the married state erased such irregularities from your mind?'

'You're being difficult,' she remonstrated, but was unable to suppress a smile. 'The fact is, if Ruth Geraghty had a child I hardly think her father would have allowed her to remain unmarried. And even if she held out against him, what's she doing in the States with the daughter over here in Newcastle? I mean, what the hell's going *on*?'

'Anything else?'

'If you'd finished the article, which you obviously haven't, you'd have seen there's quite a bit about the transactions with Morcomb Estates. *You* get a mention—look, here is it: *prominent local solicitor*—'

'Ha!'

'And there's quite a bit about Sedleigh Hall and my father and the estate before he died . . . I mean, what's all that got to do with the kidnapping of that poor child?'

Eric shrugged. 'Nothing, but they clearly want to pad out the article when the news content is so thin. It accounts for Geraghty's presence in England, after all.'

'Well, I'm not sure I like our names being thrown in the ring in this way. Besides, they could have got some of this information only from Geraghty, or his advisers. I mean, the meeting and the shooting party at Sedleigh Hall, they weren't exactly known all over the North-East, were they?'

'Some judicious ferreting—'

'Liam Geraghty,' Anne said firmly, 'did not strike me as the kind of man who talked easily about his own business. So why has he been so free with it now?'

'Upset, distraught . . .'

'Hmmm.' Anne wriggled, slipping her left leg across his, nestling down into the chair with him. 'I still think there's something odd about the report.'

'You've a suspicious mind,' Eric said and put down his drink. He kissed her lightly on the forearm, and then more positively on her throat.

She murmured in deep satisfaction, 'I do have a suspicious mind. About what you have on *your* mind.'

'Entirely innocent.'

'You hands aren't . . . We'll be called in to dinner soon. It's duck.'

'It can wait.'

'It can't. Besides, I thought an old man like you only did this sort of thing in bed.'

Eric leaned back and glared at her in mock anger. 'You're determined to have me analyse this newspaper story, aren't you?'

'If it keeps your mind off disgraceful behaviour before dinner!'

'All right, I agree with you, it's odd, but maybe Ruth

Geraghty uses her father's name because she prefers it to
the name of the child's father. And maybe you're exaggerat-
ing the whole thing just because you've met Geraghty, and
like him—'

'I think he's smashing,' she giggled. 'So *manly*!'

'In which case,' Eric said coolly, sliding away from her,
'I'll tell you what's *really* odd. How come the newspaper
hasn't stated whether she was married or not? There are
registers of births, deaths and marriages. So why aren't they
more specific?'

'There! You *are* intrigued! Why can't you be more honest
with me?'

'I was going to be. You insisted on dinner first.'

It was a curious situation, nevertheless. As Anne had said,
it was the things that were missing from the account that
were intriguing. It would have been a relatively simple
matter for the journalist who wrote the piece to make a
quick check to discover not only whether Ruth Geraghty
had married, but also the identity of the husband. Equally,
the lack of explanation regarding the girl's presence on
Tyneside pointed to repression on someone's part: journal-
ists rarely failed to follow up issues like that. Particularly if
they *were* issued.

There was something else that lurked at the back of Eric's
mind during the next few days. He had the feeling he was
missing something. He was not centrally concerned with
the Geraghty business but it kept returning to his mind. It
might have been something he himself had said, or maybe
it was something to do with a look, an impression, an
attitude out of character. He could not pin it down and he
felt irritated when it intruded upon his thoughts in the office,
when he should have been concentrating upon other things,
like the Turriff prosecution. After all, the kidnapping was
none of his business.

But then, on the Friday morning it became his business.
He had hoped to have a couple of hours to himself to

wrestle with some of the new tax legislation that had emerged. It was easy to get rusty on such matters, and he had at least three files for counsel briefing on tax matters, largely won as a result of his success some years earlier with the affairs of Lord Morcomb. Tax files could be lucrative, and he was insistent upon his independence from Anne's money. It was with a feeling of suppressed irritation, therefore, that he picked up the phone in response to the call from reception.

'Yes, Frances?'

'I'm sorry to interrupt you, Mr Ward, but there's a gentleman here in the office who wants to make an appointment.'

'Can't you fix one for him?'

There was a brief hesitation. 'He says it's urgent, and he really would like to see you immediately.'

'What's his name?'

For a moment Eric thought it might be Phil Heckles, changing his mind over prosecuting Detective-Superintendent Mason. But he was wrong. 'It's a Mr Cullen.'

Cullen . . . Cullen . . . The man in the flat, one of the group who were in with the loan shark Sam Turriff. He'd refused to help, got angry. Now he would have changed his mind for some reason.

Eric hesitated, glanced at the papers in front of him and then sighed. 'All right. Ask him to come up in about five minutes.'

The papers had been cleared away and the desk top was tidy when, five minutes later, Tony Cullen entered the room. He had obviously been sleeping badly. His light blue eyes were dark-shadowed, a mingling of anger, frustration and despair. His mouth had been stubborn when first Eric had met him; now it was marked with doubt and his edginess was apparent from the way in which he refused the offer of a chair but remained standing, hands thrust deep into the pockets of his cheap leather jacket, shifting his weight from one foot to another, a runner ready to sprint if only he knew where the finishing line was.

'Mr Cullen. You said you needed to see me urgently.'

'That's right.'

'Turriff's been putting pressure on you?'

'Turriff?' His glance became glazed with incomprehension at a time when perhaps he comprehended nothing. He half turned, stared down at the busy Quayside, and then turned back to face Eric, his brow furrowed and anxious. 'I didn't come to talk about Turriff. To hell with that. I'll let you have what you want . . . No, it's not Turriff.'

'Why do you wish to see me?'

'It's my daughter.'

There was a short silence. Something cold touched the back of Eric's neck. 'What about your daughter?'

'Kate.'

Eric recognized the pain and panic in Tony Cullen's eyes, and instinctively he knew. 'You'd better sit down.'

'You don't understand. I'm getting nowhere! They won't talk to me, they won't help me—but *it's my daughter who's been snatched!*'

Eric rose. Puppet-like, Cullen reached out for the chairback, pulled it sideways towards him, and sat down helplessly. Eric stared at him for several seconds. The man's face seemed to have crumpled, creased with uncertainty, unmade by the pressure of events he could not explain. Eric sat down again. 'Liam Geraghty—'

'He's my bloody father-in-law.'

Cullen's tone was fierce; it was clear there was little love lost between him and Geraghty.

'The name of Cullen wasn't mentioned in the newspaper reports,' Eric said slowly,

'That's Geraghty's doing.'

'Why?'

'He hates me. Took his precious daughter from him.'

Eric frowned, leaned back in his chair and observed Cullen thoughtfully. Emotionally, the man seemed to be falling apart. He was unable to keep his hands still, and his glance flickered around the room restlessly, unable to settle. On the other hand, the reaction was hardly surprising: his daughter Kate had been kidnapped. But Eric was unable to understand the relationship with Geraghty.

'I'm not quite clear what you want,' Eric said slowly. 'Your daughter has been kidnapped, and I imagine the police will be doing all they can to get her back. Liam Geraghty too—he'll be anxious to get Kate back. So what do you want from me?'

Cullen's glance settled on Eric; it held elements of desperation. 'But that's the point. Geraghty will have got at the police. They'll be looking for Kate, oh aye, but will they find her? And me, I'm her father but I'm shoved in the background, and no one is talking to me and I'm not being told what's going on. Hysterical they say, don't get hysterical! *But she's my kid!*'

Eric thought for a moment. Cullen's words were wild, but perhaps he should not dismiss them too lightly. The man would have good reason for seeking a solicitor, at a time when his efforts should have been directed towards working with the local police to recover his daughter. 'You say Liam Geraghty . . . hates you. I think maybe you should tell me all about it, why you think that way. Let's go right back to the beginning. You married Geraghty's daughter. How did you get to meet her?'

Cullen looked at his hands, fingers twisting together. 'I was brought up in Sunderland. Got a job on the Tyne, in the shipyards. Before they closed down, that was. I was twenty then, like. One day I was coming out of the yard, been working a late shift, and I saw this girl. She was sitting up on the bank, sketching. Looking out across the Tyne, and the sun was low in the sky. Reddish colour, sort of glow to her hair.'

There was more than nostalgia in his tone as it dropped, more than loss. Whatever had driven the couple apart, it would have been something Cullen would have resisted.

'She had come over from Ireland. Geraghty, he wasn't too pleased about it but she was always a strong-willed girl, and she didn't want to get tied up in the business world he'd developed. That got up his nose, you knaa? But he had to give in, though he wouldn't have liked her settlin' for a course in Fashion Design at Newcastle Polytechnic. He'd wanted her to go to University. But she knew what she wanted.'

He turned his head, glanced briefly out of the window as though the words had drifted there, and among them was something he wished to recall. 'Knew what she wanted, aye, she knew that. It became *me*, after a little while. Didn't understand it, at first; I thought maybe it was just the summer, and the fell—we used to go walking weekends, up above Otterburn, there. But it got serious, certainly for me, and when she talked about her old man I got worried. Then she asked us to marry her. Just like that. So we got married. Geraghty played hell. But there was nothing he could do.'

'You didn't go back to Ireland?' Eric asked.

Cullen shook his head. 'He wanted us to. I'd have gone. Let's be honest, Mr Ward: I was working in the yards, but I knew from the rumours it wouldn't be long before I was sent up the road. And Geraghty, though he didn't like the idea of Ruth marrying like that, once it was done he'd have made the best of it. Given me a job in his company, something like that.'

'It didn't suit Ruth?'

'Absolutely. She was dead against going back to Ireland. Said it would be a kind of failure, and now she was free of her old man there was no way she wanted to be beholden to him again. I didn't quite follow that, but it it was what she wanted, that was fair enough with me. So we got a small place up near the Leazes and things were okay for a while. Then she got pregnant.'

'Kate?'

'That's right.' Cullen wrinkled his nose in self-doubt, grimacing as he sought out old reasons for past actions.

'Geraghty rang me, gave me a right bollocking. He was mad as hell, thought I'd forced the child on her. But that wasn't the way of it. Ruth *wanted* a kid, it was her idea, and me, well, I just went along with it, you knaa? I was still working then, there seemed to be no problem. But then, afterwards, it all changed.'

'How do you mean?'

'She got restless during the time she was pregnant. She didn't finish the course at the Poly and she seemed at a loose end. Maybe the flat got her down; maybe she began to hanker after Ireland. I don't know. All I do know is that once the baby was born there was a few weeks when everything was great and then she began to change.'

'She became restless?'

Cullen shook his head. 'Not just that. Bitter, like. Took to swearing about Geraghty, arguing he should have done better by her. Then she calmed down again, and we rubbed along well enough for a year or so, and she went back to finish her course at the Poly. Took her longer than I'd expected. I was at work during the day. She got someone in to look after Kate. She was out, friends at the college, and there was parties . . .'

His voice died away, and he stared at his hands again. They were shaking slightly. He was saying things, but there were things that were not being said. Eric could guess at the situation. Young girl, affluent background, marrying a young shipyard worker in a glow of romantic love. Even the pregnancy would have been sought as an excitement, a fulfilment. The aftermath removed the romanticism. A restrictive life, claustrophobic premises, a crying child, opportunities for self-fulfilment lost. She would have money of her own, and would perhaps be contemptuous of the amount her husband brought home. She could afford to pay for someone to look after Kate, and she could seize the chance to pick up again the possibilities she had discarded. But the return to college life hardly eased things: old friends, new friends, and none of them like Tony Cullen, most of them carefree, bound into the world of fashion, edging her into student life again, free from restrictions. And all the time comparing Tony Cullen, a shipyard worker with no future, with the heady excitements of the expensive, unreal world of fashion.

'When did you get divorced?' Eric asked gently.

Cullen shrugged. 'About five, six years ago.'

'Did Ruth get custody of Kate?'

Something flared in Tony Cullen's face. He sat up in the chair, glared briefly at Eric and shook his head. 'You don't understand. That wasn't the way it was. She didn't *want* Kate.'

'How do you mean?'

'She got the divorce in the States. She hadn't seen Kate for maybe three years then. There was never any question at that time of her wanting her daughter. I was bringing up Kate, the way I've always brought her up.'

'So when did she go to the States?'

'Ah, it was about two years after she finished at the college. Things were bad between us. I never saw much of her and there was this woman who came in during the day, and I got fed up with it all and there was blazin' rows. Then she got this offer down in London, working with some department store and she wanted us to move but there was no way I was leavin' the North-East, you knaa? She didn't put up much fight when I insisted Kate stayed with me, and she was earning good money, used to send us a bit, like.' Cullen turned his face away, shamed by his own admission, a northern man being supported by his wife. 'I was out of work then, and the bairn needed the money.'

'And after London?'

'She never really came back to us. Went her own way. Used to drop in couple of times a year, like a bloody cyclone, kiss the kid and gone. Kate never really knew who the hell she was, believe me. Then she was off to the States, and we didn't see her at all for three years.'

'What about Liam Geraghty all this time?'

Cullen frowned, trying to think back, understand motives and events. 'Difficult. He came over a few times, saw the bairn, but never seemed much interested. If it had been a boy now . . . he wanted a boy, I reckon. He used to stand off in the flat, nostrils curled up, you knaa? Like he didn't want to be there, but duty called. He got rid of the duty by shoving a regular fifty quid a month to us. I didn't want it, but I was out of work . . .' The words hurt him, and his mouth grew rigid, angry with an anger directed at himself as well as at Liam Geraghty. 'He was never really interested, not properly. They were a pair, Ruth and her old man. Cold. The bairn meant nothing. And then suddenly she came back and things got bad.'

'She returned to the North-East?'

Cullen nodded. 'London first, then Edinburgh, and then Manchester. The company down there had interests in the North-East and she took to visiting Tyneside. And suddenly she was all over us. It was suffocating. Kate was just ten years old and I think maybe Ruth saw her dressed up, an accessory to her own personality, you knaa? She *wanted* her, and now that most of the messy, difficult business of growing up was over she could *use* her.'

'I hardly think—'

'I'm *telling* you, Mr Ward,' Cullen insisted fiercely. 'She was talking about using her in fashion displays and all that sort of crap. She'd have ruined the kid!'

Eric hesitated. If Cullen was right in his statements he was inclined to agree. But there would be another viewpoint: father out of work, child benefiting from a different lifestyle. 'Did Ruth make any formal attempt to get custody of Kate?'

'She did,' Cullen said grimly. 'She went back to the States that summer, got a lawyer to set up a hearing. They told her it would have to be done here, in England. We'd been divorced about two years then. So she came back, took out proceedings.'

'Wardship proceedings, I presume, since no custody decision had been ordered on divorce.'

'Aye, something like that, I never did get the hang of it all,' Cullen said. 'Anyway, they said some hard things in court, her and her lawyer.'

'But you got custody.'

'I told the truth!' Cullen's tone was bitter, hard-edged with malice. 'I told them exactly what had happened and why. I didn't owe her anything any more, and if Liam Geraghty didn't like me telling the court what a whore his daughter was, that was his problem! She'd never married again but she'd had men before and since our divorce, and the way she moved around the country, here and in the States, it would have been no life for a child! Yes, I got custody and I got something else too, and it really stuck in Geraghty's gullet!'

'What was that?' Eric asked, but already guessing.

'I got a court order, making her pay us a monthly allowance.'

There was a short silence, broken only by the rasping sound of Cullen's breathing. Eric had expected the decision of the court: unemployed, with a wife making considerable sums of money and with a wealthy background in addition, Cullen had a good case for maintenance once it was agreed that the child was better off with him. Custody usually went to the mother, and maintenance was usually paid to her by the father, but the court was not averse to reversing the situation where the facts demanded it. The primary consideration was always the welfare of the child.

'When was all this finalized?'

'About two years ago. She appealed, of course. It cost her. She lost. Kate stayed with me.'

'What *about* Kate?'

Cullen knew what he meant. His eyes were hooded momentarily, concealing his own defensiveness, the doubts that would always lie inside his head about whether he had done what was right. 'She . . . she's taken it all well. She always wanted to stay with me. Ruth never fooled her, coming back out of nowhere, making all sorts of promises. Kate's got her head screwed on the right way. She knew she was best off with me.' He paused, shook his head slightly as though admitting to himself that nothing was black and white and simple. 'That's not to say she wasn't tempted. Best thing for her would have been me and Ruth back together again, but that'll never happen. And when Ruth spoke to her, her eyes used to shine, she'd light up . . . Ah, man, it was wrong, Ruth should never have come back. Kate got . . . quiet, you knaa? Reserved, when it was all over.'

The room fell silent. Outside, above the Quayside, gulls wheeled noisily in the sunlit air, dipping beneath the steel frame of the Tyne Bridge, sliding down in long planings to the freighters moored at Pandon. In Eric's office Tony Cullen had reviewed his past and was hurting as he considered his own weaknesses, his own wrongs, reflected in the submissiveness of his daughter's personality. His words had blamed Ruth Geraghty, but inside he would be blaming himself, just as much.

Gently Eric Ward said, 'None of this explains why your daughter has now disappeared.'

Cullen's head came up. 'It does. Ruth's got her.'

Eric hesitated for a few moment, then, carefully, he said, 'If you said this to the police, they would have certainly investigated the possibility.'

'No. Geraghty.'

'You mean he's persuaded them otherwise?'

'I mean the whole damn thing is a fix! I told you, Mr Ward, I'm entitled to custody of Kate. I got no money of my own. Some time ago, it must have been eight months ago, the money from the States dried up. Ruth stopped paying. That was all right with me: I never wanted the damned money anyway! It was just a way of my getting at her, I admit that now. But the money stopped, I was still out of work apart from the odd bit of casual labour, and I had to take a loan from Sam Turriff and his ticket-man. School clothes . . . the bairn needed them. But the silence from the States, and then, when Ruth came over six months ago and didn't even get in touch, I was puzzled, wondered what was going on in her head. Now I know! Now I know what she was up to. She was planning to steal Kate away from me!'

'Mr Cullen—'

'No, believe me! Look, she's got a boyfriend over here. Name of Maxwell. They may even be thinking of getting wed, I don't know. She wants Kate. She's been mad as hell at the result of the custody hearings. And Geraghty—that bastard never likes losing anything, and now Ruth has made her own way, built up her own business, she's the apple of his eye again, and they're close as they ever were. There's just the one thing been spoiling things for them.'

Eric could understand. Ruth and her father would want Tony Cullen erased from their sensibilities, but that could never happen while Kate was still on Tyneside.

'Do you have any proof of what you suspect?' Eric asked.

'Proof? That's police business, not mine.' Cullen clenched and unclenched his fist in a gesture of angry despair. 'Look, man, when I heard that Kate had disappeared I went straight around to the coppers and they reacted. I mean, they got skates on, and took statements, sent a couple of Pandas out and went whizzin' around the City, making all sorts of inquiries. I mean, they acted as though they *cared*. But over the weekend it changed. They got in touch with Geraghty and he came charging in and suddenly they didn't want to know me no more. I been around there, but all I get is soft words, they're making inquiries, they're doing all that's possible—*but they haven't found Kate!* And time's slipping past. There was no announcement, no newspaper story because the first thing they said was they wanted to wait, not scare anyone into stupid actions, wait for a contact—but after they talk to Geraghty there *is* an announcement and I'm not even mentioned!'

Carefully Eric asked, 'What do you think the reason for that might be?'

Tony Cullen glared at him with glazed eyes. 'It's obvious,

isn't it? The whole emphasis upon the thing in the newspaper is that it's Geraghty's granddaughter who's been kidnapped, not my daughter! The stress is on money, Geraghty's money. It screams out at you, man. Kate's been kidnapped because Geraghty can pay to have her brought back.'

'Which you can't. It's a natural supposition, and a natural bias for a news story.'

'You're missing the point, Mr Ward! It's really just a con, an attempt to divert attention away from the truth. There's not going to be any ransom demand on Geraghty. He's saying he expects one to be made, and that's how the story is coming out and that's why the police are playing quiet with me. But there'll be no demand because it's Ruth who's snatched Kate, and Geraghty knows it, and all he's doing is playing for time until Kate can be whipped off to the States where I can't get hold of her. I mean, dammit, once she's there, what will I be able to do? I got no money; there's no bloody way I could afford a fight to bring her back!'

The man was bleeding inside, emotionally panic-stricken, scared that he had lost his daughter for ever. Eric sat back, thinking. There was logic in what Cullen had had to say, sense in some of his suppositions. In many ways, additionally, it was to be hoped that he was right and that Geraghty was involved. That way, at least, there could be no doubts about the girl's safety and general well-being. Eric leaned forward across his desk. 'What is it you want me to do, Mr Cullen?'

'I . . . I came to you because we met the other day . . . I'm not used to lawyers, you seemed . . . different. I want my daughter back, Mr Ward; I don't want to lose her. I want you to help, stop Geraghty and Ruth taking her to the States. And then I'll help you any way I can over the Turriff business—'

'There's no need for a bargain, Mr Cullen,' Eric said. 'And I'll do all I can to help you get Kate back—from whoever's got her.'

*

There were details to be obtained. Eric got most of them from Tony Cullen during the course of the next hour. Cullen had no car, had wanted Kate to go to a school with a rather better reputation than the one in his own locality, so had reached an arrangement with a Mrs Chaddha, whose own young children attended a school nearby. Each morning, Kate had been picked up by Mrs Chaddha and dropped off at the school; each evening, after picking up her own children Mrs Chaddha had gone on to collect Kate, and bring her to the end of the road in which the estate was located. Cullen was always there, waiting for her when she got home, as he had been the day Eric had called to see him.

On the Friday, when she had not returned, he had made his way into the street to see Mrs Chaddha driving towards him. She was in a state of hysterical panic. She gave him a garbled story of a car, someone picking up Kate and bundling her into the vehicle, minutes before her own arrival. They had gone straight to the police. A search had been started, immediately.

Cullen had no idea if Ruth was in England. She had been on Tyneside some months previously. His belief now was that she had been present then to plan the kidnapping of her daughter. Her boyfriend was a man called Peter Maxwell. He was a Tyneside businessman, who was involved with the development of computer software in some way. He occasionally visited the States; Cullen thought that the man had probably met Kate when Ruth had been over to England and taken the girl out with her for a treat. Cullen had never objected to such excursions: he had never expected recent events.

The attitude of the police seemed to have changed on Saturday afternoon. Cullen had seen Geraghty arrive but they had not spoken. Since then there had been what Cullen described as a wall of silence between him and the police. They had been sympathetic, but unhelpful.

Eric promised to be in touch with him as quickly as he could, after he had made certain inquiries.

Once Tony Cullen had left the office the taxation files, inevitably, remained disregarded. Unsettled, Eric turned to the statute book to refresh his memory. If Cullen was right, Geraghty would be guilty of an offence—that of child stealing—under an old Act: the Offences Against the Person Act 1861. And Ruth, as mother of the child? If she was directly involved, or for that matter indirectly, she too could be committing an offence. He read the dry, stilted language of the Act. *'Unlawfully ... by force ... take away ... any child under the age of fourteen years, with intent to deprive any parent of possession of such child.'*

An unlawful act. The stark words covered much more than the act itself: they concerned human passions, emotions, some of the most basic of human feelings.

Eric snapped the volume closed. He walked to the window and stood staring out, unseeingly, at the river winding its way eastwards, a black, glinting snake. He did not normally touch matrimonial matters in his business. They were too painful and too messy. Moreover, they struck chords perhaps too close to home. He could still remember the sight of his first wife's contorted face, her body pinned by that of her lover's ... And unbidden, another scene stole into his mind: Anne, on the fells, holding on possessively to a young lawyer's arm. Mark Fenham, much the same age as Anne ...

Irritably, Eric turned away. He was aware of a familiar prickling behind his eyes, signs of an old, returning tension. Suspicion could breed such tension, and suspicion could damage irretrievably.

He had Cullen to concentrate on, and a small girl called Kate, pushed into a reserved shyness by an environment she could not understand, a glossy, exciting mother and a father who cared for her, deeply, and to whom she owed all the loyalties of her childhood.

In the morning, Eric decided, he would make a start.

CHAPTER 3

1

An early morning call brought Jackie Parton to the Quayside office where Eric was able to explain what he wanted. Parton knew the back streets of Newcastle and was accepted as a local celebrity: he would be able to act more effectively than Eric in terms of making inquiries about what actually happened when Kate Cullen had been kidnapped. As for Eric, he had two calls to make. The first was to the police.

Once he had cleared his desk and told Lizzie that he would not be available for the rest of the day Eric made his first contact, a man he had rated as a friend in the past. The greeting he received, once he made known the reason for his call, was muted, but he received a name nevertheless: Detective-Inspector Bannon. An appointment was fixed for eleven-thirty that morning.

Eric arrived in good time. He was shown to a small waiting-room and some twenty minutes later he was asked to step into the office across the corridor. He had not met Bannon previously: the detective-inspector turned out to be a lean, poker-faced man with thinning hair and an occupational caution when questioned. He agreed he was in charge of the investigation into the kidnapping of Kate Cullen, but was reluctant to discuss it, even when told that Eric was acting on behalf of the child's father.

Eric was beginning to feel angry with frustration after some ten minutes verbal fencing with Bannon when the door behind him opened. He turned his head. Framed in the doorway was a man he recognized, and one whom he disliked actively.

'Good morning, Ward.'

'Good morning, Mason.'

'Mind if I sit in?' Mason asked Bannon. 'Got an interest in this case, Bob.'

Bannon seemed relieved that his superior officer was prepared to give his time. Eric stared at Detective-Superintendent Mason for several seconds, puzzled why the man should wish to be present. Mason twisted his fleshy mouth into a semblance of a smile but it held neither warmth nor humour. He settled himself comfortably in a chair to Eric's right, slightly out of line of sight but able to watch Eric closely. 'Carry on, Bob,' he said graciously.

'It was Mr Ward who was talking,' Bannon said in a cautious tone.

'And I was saying that I found it odd that rather less than cooperation is presently being granted to the legal representative of the child's father.'

'Cullen?' Mason said. 'What cooperation are you asking for? We've got a number of officers on the case, haven't we, Bob?'

'Three,' Bannon muttered.

'Not very much seems to have been achieved,' Eric said coldly.

'Not much to go on,' Bannon replied.

'There's been no ransom demand, you see,' Mason interrupted. 'We've talked to people at the scene, made the usual inquiries—'

'There are no *usual* inquiries in a case like this,' Eric snapped.

'—but so far we've come up with nothing. We're keeping our ears to the ground, but until we get a positive lead—'

'You're doing nothing.'

Mason was a big man. His hair was greying at the temples but was thick and black elsewhere and he sported a thin moustache. His eyes were heavily pouched, almost sleepy in appearance, and his face was fleshy. His skin was becoming blotchy now, as he tried to contain a slow irritation. It might have arisen as a result of Eric's sharp comment, but it was likely there were other, older reasons, both for his shortness of temper and his presence at this interview.

'Now look, Ward, just because you were a copper years ago it doesn't give you the right to march in here and query the tactics we're using. We're playing things carefully, because this is a delicate case: young kid snatched, possibly lot of money involved—'

'Liam Geraghty's money?'

'It's his granddaughter.'

'But you've received no ransom call. Geraghty's working closely with you, of course.'

'Naturally.'

'And he thinks there will be a ransom call?'

Mason's sleepy eyes moved over Eric thoughtfully. Behind his desk Detective-Inspector Bannon sat stiffly, accepting the role Mason was assuming in the discussion. Mason nodded at last. 'He does. And so do we.'

'You've considered no other possibilities?'

'Such as?'

'You are aware,' Eric said coldly, 'that Ruth Cullen and the father of the child are divorced?'

'Ruth *Geraghty*. Yes, we're aware.'

'And that the father obtained custody of Kate.'

'What are you getting at, Ward?'

'Oh, come on, Mason, don't tell me you haven't considered the possibility that the kidnapping was undertaken by the mother, in an attempt to get the child back with her to the States?'

'There's no evidence—'

'I'm talking about investigative possibilities. It seems to me you're blinding yourself, because Liam Geraghty is involved, to the fact there may never be a ransom note because ransom was never in the wind.'

'Ward—'

'Why, for instance, have you virtually ignored the existence of my client, Cullen? Why has he not been mentioned in newspaper statements? Why is the emphasis maintained upon an investigation that may be based on a false premise?

Why am I being faced by a non-cooperative attitude, as my client has been these last few days?'

Mason straightened in his chair. His breathing had quickened and the mottling of his face was now more evident. He glanced quickly towards the passive Bannon, behind his desk. 'Bob,' he said thickly, 'I think I can handle this from now on. You can leave us.'

Bannon rose to his feet without a word. He barely glanced at Eric before he left the room. After he had gone Mason rose and prowled heavily around the room for a few moments, hands locked behind his back, before he made his way behind the desk, and took the chair Dieter had vacated. He faced Eric, one hand on his chin, fingers caressing his dark moustache. 'You're out of line, Ward.'

'I'm stating situations as I see them.'

'You know how the Force works. There are lines we follow, routines we have—'

'This case isn't routine.'

The fleshy mouth moved angrily. 'You got no say in what is or isn't routine, and you got no reason to suggest we're not doing things that need to be done. You think you can charge in here and make accusations—'

'You haven't answered my questions, Mason.'

'Nor do I bloody well intend to, Ward!' Mason's eyes were hard, anger moving in their depths as he glared at Eric. 'The fact is, I got better things to do than to come in here and listen to your complaints and answer your thinly veiled accusations. We've got two major cases on our hands right now: this kidnapping, with Geraghty breathing down our necks, and a drug-smuggling business in from Teesside. Two major cases, and I'm sure we'll get the kid back, in time, same as we'll nail the bastards who brought the heroin in *and* the bastard who stole the stuff from under our noses.'

'I heard about the drug business. Let's hope you get better luck—or more efficient—with the kidnapping.'

Mason stood up abruptly, losing control of an anger that would have been simmering inside him long before he even entered the room. 'I don't have to take that kind of sneer from you, Ward! I'm well aware of what you think of me— you hate my guts, the way I hate yours! I always thought you were rubbish when you were on the beat with me; you never had the guts to stand up and be counted, put the yobboes against the wall and show them who was in charge, the only way the bastards understand. You were soft then, and you're still soft! Trouble is, you're in a position now to cause trouble of a different kind with your softness. That Heckles business—you know that bastard's a junkie who's been on skag for years. If I'd had a few more hours with him . . . Instead, you make a fool of me in court, and get him out—'

'If he took my advice he'd bring charges—'

'Listen, *Mister* Solicitor Ward,' Mason growled, raising one admonitory finger and prodding it in Eric's direction, 'you want to be careful! I'm up to the gills with you right now, you and your bloody pussyfooting ways! I'll have your blood if you cross my path again over Heckles, and first chance I get to pull him in I'll spread his nose all over his face. Stay off my back, Ward! And stay out of this kidnapping business. It's none of your affair!'

'My client—'

'*Client*,' Mason sneered. 'What're you *talking* about? A broken-down good-for-nothing, no job, no bloody sense— how's he going to pay you? What can he—or you—do to get the kid back? Geraghty's the grandfather: he wants the kid back, and we'll do it for him. So stay out of the way, don't muddy waters, don't hinder the investigation, and tell Cullen that if he's not careful maybe we can pull him inside on something or other, too.'

Mason had suddenly gone too far, and he knew it. He glared at Eric, his face suffused with anger, and sat down abruptly. Eric stared at him. 'You're not concerned about this case,' he said quietly. 'You're just concerned about staying the right side of Liam Geraghty.'

'You've had your time, Ward.'

'You came in here to have a go at me, and also to get Bannon off the hook. You're doing *nothing* over Kate Cullen's kidnapping!'

'I said, you've had all the time you're entitled to. If you, or your *client*, don't like the way we're handling things with Mr Geraghty . . . *sue* us!'

The sneering confidence with which Detective-Superintendent Mason had dismissed him was disturbing. Eric could understand the anger the man felt about the Heckles affair, possibly sharpened by the failure of the police to prevent the fiasco that had developed over the Teesside drug-smuggling episode—although, Eric guessed, that had been exacerbated by the fact that three different Forces had been involved. The co-ordination of the Northumbria, Durham and Teesside Forces could have led to problems.

Even so, the fact that Mason seemed unworried at any possible repercussions over the Kate Cullen kidnapping and the treatment of Tony Cullen was surprising. It suggested to Eric that maybe officers senior to Mason had been brought into the matter. That would give Mason the confidence to beat away criticism.

Eric made his way across town and parked in the multi-storey car park. It was only a short walk from there to Grey Street and the offices of Maxwell Computer Services, Ltd. Eric could have parked at the Quayside near the office and walked up the hill, but since he'd be driving north after his interview with Maxwell there seemed to be little point.

The offices were high-ceilinged, central, well-groomed and air-conditioned. The secretary in the outer office was equally well-groomed and equally cool. When she finally allowed him in to see her employer it was with a level of trained condescension that put him in the role of suppliant.

The handshake in the other room could not have been warmer.

Peter Maxwell was six feet tall and built like an athlete. His hair was dark and wavy, cut to a fashionable length.

He had perfect planes to his face and a trick of holding himself so that it was apparent. He moved with the elegant grace of a model in a television advertisement, and he had chosen his clothing to make the most of his light blue eyes: blue shirt, dark blue tie emblazoned with a cricket club motif, dark blue suit. His teeth were white, expensive capped perfection. 'Mr Ward . . . What can I do to help you?' He had a deep voice, rich with the sincerity of a man who wants to help. He had a likeable smile. Eric didn't like him.

'I represent a Mr Antony Cullen,' Eric said bluntly.

'Ah . . .' The smile hardly wavered. Maxwell turned, waved Eric to the expensive leather chair by the glass-topped coffee table and sat down beside him, one long, elegant leg crossed over the other. 'Cullen . . . I'd assumed you'd come on business.'

'What exactly is your business, Mr Maxwell?'

'Computer software mainly,' Maxwell replied eagerly. 'I've come in on the back of the boom, if you like. Not talent; not even hard work.' The modesty of his smile belied the statement.

'You've been in business long?'

'Seven years. We've done well. Made a name for ourselves in the North-East, and picked up some good international contracts through our London agency, too. But nothing stands still . . .' He continued for a little while, explaining to Eric the ramifications of international computer contracts, the rapidly developing demand for software, and how the British were now regarded as the leaders in software development, even if their chances of leading in computer hardware were now remote. 'So, as far as we're concerned, the world's the oyster and it's time we expanded overseas.'

'Where, precisely?' Eric asked.

The blue eyes fixed calmly on his. 'America. The land of opportunity.'

'What sort of operation will you open up there?'

'The same.'

'And this company?'

'We'll probably close down. Might hold on for a while. But the . . . opportunities in the States are much more promising.'

'I understand you know Ruth Geraghty.'

There was a short silence. Peter Maxwell swung his elegant leg thoughtfully, contemplating the pale blue socks he wore as though they could answer his problem. Not that he was admitting to a problem. 'Ruth . . . Yes, I'm a friend of Ruth Geraghty . . . and I'm aware she was married to Cullen.'

'You're also aware her daughter's been kidnapped?'

'Of course.'

'Has Ruth been in touch with you about it?'

The hesitation was brief. 'I last spoke to Ruth—on the phone—about ten days ago.'

'Before the kidnapping. And you've not been in touch since? I find that surprising.'

'Why?'

'In view of the closeness of your relationship.'

Some of the charm left Maxwell's eyes. His voice took on a harder edge. 'I don't think the nature of my relationship is a matter for discussion between us, Mr Ward. Nor the question of what she and I might discuss on the phone.' His natural control reasserted itself. 'On the other hand, I can add that Ruth is a businesswoman. She travels a great deal. This . . . business will have been a shock to her. She would not naturally turn to me . . . rather, I would guess, to Liam Geraghty.'

'She travels . . . Is she in England now?'

'I haven't seen her.'

'Is she with her father?'

'I haven't seen him for two months.'

'You answer questions like a politician, Mr Maxwell.'

'I'm a simple businessman, not a politician.' Maxwell smiled lazily, enjoying himself. 'And I really don't see how I can help you, Mr Ward.'

'I'm not sure how you can either,' Eric conceded, 'unless

you can tell me anything about the reason for the kidnapping of Kate Cullen.'

'Why should I be able to tell you anything about that?'

'Because her father is certain that the kidnapping was done by Ruth.'

'That's preposterous.'

'Cullen doesn't think so.'

'Cullen is an impecunious oaf.'

Maxwell had made no attempt to disguise the contempt in his voice. For perhaps the first time the real man was shining through. Eric stared at him dispassionately, weighing up how he could make him expose himself further. 'When do you intend to go to the States?'

'End of the month. There are certain deals to tie up. Then, I'll be able to—'

'Go out and marry Ruth Geraghty?'

Maxwell paused. He uncrossed his legs, leaned back in his chair. 'My personal business—'

'Might become affected. Your plans might be curtailed.'

'What's that supposed to mean?'

Eric smiled. 'I can't be specific, because I don't know the facts, not all of them. But the hypothesis that Mr Cullen has put to me is that Ruth's kidnapped Kate to get her back to the States. You've met the child, I gather. Would you be happy having her in your family?'

Slightly nettled, Maxwell said, 'I've not admitted that Ruth and I—'

'But let's assume,' Eric interrupted affably, 'that you and Ruth *are* going to get married. I've no doubt Liam Geraghty will be prepared to put money into your business venture in the States—you'd be his son-in-law, after all, and one of whom he'd approve rather more than he did Tony Cullen. And it would be *nice* under such circumstances to have Kate with you both. You could give her so much better an upbringing. California, isn't it? Isn't that where there are such great opportunities for software development?'

'You're making too many assumptions, Mr Ward.'

'Hypothesis only, I assure you. But let's assume for a moment that Mr Cullen is right, and Ruth has kidnapped her own daughter. It's pretty clear Liam Geraghty would give her support. But wouldn't you, too?'

Maxwell was silent. He stared at Eric, slightly baffled by the veiled attack. He was not ready, nor built for this kind of tension, and he was ruffled.

'Circumstances such as these,' Eric went on, 'could cause you a problem. Because, hypothetically speaking, if you *are* involved in the snatching of Kate Cullen, you ought to be quite clear about the possible consequences.'

'Now look here—'

'You see, there's a sort of myth prevalent that if it's the *parent* who snatches the child, there can be no criminal prosecution. It's the result of the proviso to Section 56 of the Offences Against the Person Act 1861. Forgive me for sounding so legalistic. But the proviso says that a parent claiming possession of the child will be immune from prosecution. Oh, there might be a citation for contempt of a court order, but there'll be no *prosecution*. Is that what they told you, Mr Maxwell?'

'No one's told me anything, Mr Ward. I've not been involved.' But the man's eyes were wary, all hint of friendliness gone.

'Well, no matter, *I'm* telling you now. I said the immunity was mythological. It's so. You see, the Court of Appeal has ruled that for a parent to use *force* to take the child from the other parent is an offence unless there is lawful excuse. Was there a lawful excuse for the snatch, Mr Maxwell?'

'This has nothing to do with me,' Maxwell muttered.

'For if there was no lawful excuse, and I see no sign of one in this instance—a loving, if penurious father—then a prosecution can follow. Not only of the parent. A prosecution will lie also against the accessories or agents of the parent. Do you know what that means?'

There was a slightly glazed look about Maxwell; he seemed to be thinking of other things.

'It means,' Eric continued softly, 'that if you *have* been involved with Ruth Geraghty in the kidnapping of her daughter you could be sent to prison. I'm not sure how that would affect the business interests you're considering expanding. I'm pretty sure how the American immigration officials would react. They don't care to have people coming in who've served terms of imprisonment. For activities involving violence.'

'There was no real . . .' Maxwell's voice died away, shakily. He stared at his hands for a few moments, then looked up. His voice was harsh now, all pretence at friendliness gone. 'I don't quite know what purpose you think has been served in coming here to see me this morning, Mr Ward. I know Cullen; I can guess he'll be distressed at losing his daughter. But he has no right to suggest I'm involved. He has no right to send you here to question me.' He stood up abruptly, towering over Eric. 'And he has no right to go around making accusations. I can afford to take him to court—'

'Are you sure?' Eric asked quietly. 'Financially, yes, but if other things came out . . .?'

'Other things?'

'Who knows?' Eric paused thoughtfully. 'You see, when you take someone to court you lose control over proceedings. Matters come to light that are often unexpected. For instance, you *tell* me you've had no contact with Ruth or with Geraghty for some time. But what if it came out that it wasn't true? Are you *certain* that it wouldn't? And your planned move to the States . . . do you already have any sort of deal with Geraghty? Then there's the actual kidnapping. What if—'

'*Listen!*' Maxwell's face was pale as he leaned over Eric and his shoulders were tense, muscle bunched as though prepared for physical struggle. 'I've had enough of this. I've already told you I can't help you in these inquiries. You've already taken up time, and I can't afford to waste any more with you. Moreover, if you take my advice—'

'Yes, Mr Maxwell,' Eric said softly.

'You'll stop bothering with all this. Drop Cullen: he's bad news. He never amounted to anything and never will. You have a practice on Tyneside. You'll never make it pay if you act for scum like Cullen.'

'Whereas if I acted for *big* people like Liam Geraghty . . .'

Maxwell was silent for a moment, glaring angrily at Eric. Then he turned abruptly, walked stiff-legged to the door and held it open. 'Important people can damage a career.'

'A threat?'

'A statement.'

Eric rose. He smiled coldly. 'It's odd how people feel they can get what they want by giving advice that's blindingly obvious . . . and productive of the very effect they don't want.'

'Ward—'

'I think we'll probably meet again, Mr Maxwell. And possibly in circumstances where you'll find it more difficult to avoid answering awkward questions . . .'

2

Mrs Chaddha had proved very helpful. A small, dark woman with three young children and a Pakistani husband who worked as a driver on the Metro, she had eyes that were veiled with mistrust and experience of prejudice, but she held her own prejudices too, and one of them was a fear of the police. She had seen too much violence in the West End to want to help anyone in a uniform, but she was prepared to talk to Jackie Parton more freely concerning the day Kate Cullen had been kidnapped.

'Well, yeh, I had a funny feeling something was goin' to happen, pet. Hindsight, mebbe, but I don't know, it was a funny day, you knaa? To start with, I always had to pick up my own kids before Patel got home from work and it was a bit of a rush, but I had this arrangement with Mr Cullen

—nice lad, always felt sorry for him—and I had the car and it was no great bother for me. And Kate was no problem, she just used to sit in the back seat, not say very much, kept herself to herself, like. But that day, when she wasn't there, and there was this couple a bit hysterical, gabbling away without really *explaining* anything, if you know what I mean.'

'What had they actually seen?'

'Bit of a fracas, like. There was this car. A big feller got out of it, chased the kid, and she tried to run away but he grabbed her, bundled her into the car, and they was away even before I got there. But by *seconds*, you knaa? I mean, that old couple they was talking there like it had happened only moments before. I must have just missed it. But I didn't see no car coming down the hill, pet, I swear it.'

'They could have turned off before the lights.'

'Aye, they could've done that. Anyway, the police then come and they spoke to me, and they went into the school next day . . . but they don't know about anythin' do they?'

'How do you mean, Mrs Chaddha?'

'Well, the teachers will help, like, but what do they know either? Some of us, possible, but who wants to talk too much to the polis?'

'You can talk to me.'

'Aye, wor Jackie, I can talk to you . . .'

Not that there had been a great deal to go on. Gossip among neighbours and parents coming to the school suggested there had been a car hanging about on previous days but none could describe it. The reason was given that there were so many others cars, picking up children . . . Something about Mrs Chaddha's remarks and a hint of evasion in her replies caused Jackie to press her. Finally, she came out with the information.

'Fact is, there's some of those cars *prowl*, you know what I mean? They're not there to pick up their own kids, but someone else's. No, not like me and Kate. They pick up some of the *older* girls, and there's always men in the cars. Friday nights, specially.'

'Why?' Jackie had asked, already knowing the answer.

'They're skaggies, aren't they? The girls, I mean. They do it to get the money so they can buy on the streets. We all know about it, but what can we do? Get a fifteen-year-old kid put inside? We turn our backs on it and make sure our own kids don't get caught up in it.'

Too many people had turned their backs on the problem. Jackie had seen how it had burgeoned in Newcastle. The massive influx of heroin into Britain from Pakistan had caused the street price to fall from £350 a gramme to less than £120. It was possible to get a 'fix' for £5, and with that kind of price word had quickly spread through the network of housing estates on Tyneside. Hundreds of young people began experimenting, the older youths agreed to become mini-dealers to support their own habit and rings were quickly established on the estates themselves and in the 'squats' set up among the decaying, abandoned houses scheduled for redevelopment.

'So none of you could describe the car that may have snatched Kate Cullen because there were always cars prowling the school gates? Come on, hinny, you can do better than that!'

A little suddenly, Mrs Chaddha had admitted that there might have been someone who could help, someone who was well enough known as a skaggie, up to talking to any car-driver in the vicinity. 'I'm not sure of her name. There's three of those kids, they give the school and the area a bad name, and we don't have nothin' to do with them. But there's one in particular, she swishes up to any car that looks likely. I'm not sure of her name . . . I think she's called Davinia.'

'You tell this to the police?'

'Come on, pet, you must be *jokin'*!'

It was Danny who had put her on to it. She looked at him now and she could see that his weight was down to about six stone, his face was covered in scars from the constant scratching, and she tried to keep well away from him as much as possible, because he was always a target for the police. And Davinia didn't want too much to do with the police. She had a life to live until she set out for the South.

She was under no illusions about Danny. He was a liar, he'd do anything for money, and he needed five or six ching bags just to keep the withdrawal symptoms at bay. When he couldn't raise the £200 a week to satisfy his needs the pains would come back and his eyes would start dribbling. He didn't even get a buzz from the habit any more: he had started injecting a year back, though he'd been too scared to do it at first and had gone to a dealer in the next street to do it for him. That was a dirty needle too, Davinia reckoned. There was no way she was going to get caught on *that* kind of hook.

But she still saw Danny occasionally. He'd got her started and he was still a useful contact. If she hadn't been able to raise any punters on a Friday night, there was always the chance that Danny—half stoned—could be persuaded to let her have a part ching bag if she let him play with her. It never got much further than that: Danny was as good as dead, she used to sneer to herself.

And there was no way she was going to go that way. No mainline stuff for her: she was no fool who was going to end up screaming in a hospital. A year and she'd be out of Tyneside, living high in the South. Till then, it was just a matter of deadening the boredom, keeping high enough to be sane, using the pawing and the thrusting to get the money and then getting a trip to forget the rest of the week.

Everyone knew chasing the dragon wasn't dangerous. You kept the menace out of the drug that way, and still enjoyed the high. You just bought a box of foil from the corner shop—and some of the bastards had already started displaying the stuff with upped prices now they knew what the teenagers bought it for. You opened up the ching bag and laid a trail of skag on the tinfoil. All it took then was a lighted match, to heat the foil from underneath. It always fascinated Davinia the way the powder changed, turning into a bead of black, glistening liquid. You tilted the foil and the black liquid would run, this way and that, a live, twisting, glinting black thing and you took the tube and you followed it, inhaling the pungent fumes through the tube, chasing the black dragon until it was spent, and you were high, and nothing much mattered any more, not even the little man who had come into the pad and pushed Danny away, thrust him to one side while he started asking her questions.

Not that Davinia had told him anything. He wasn't a cop, but he asked questions and she didn't like answering questions. She told him, in the end, about the car and the bastard who'd bruised her arm and hand. She even told him about what had happened, those two characters grabbing that snotty Cullen kid. And she'd admitted she'd seen that bruising bastard before and since. He wasn't a cop, just a little feller with warm eyes and a battered face like a horse had rolled on it.

She hadn't told him anything important. Not about the clouds, and the drifting, and the winged, spreading delights that came from chasing the dragon.

3

Nick Hawthorne was a little late for his appointment at Eric's office, and when the big, shaggy-haired civil servant entered he dropped in a chair with a weary sigh. 'What a bloody day.'

Eric smiled. 'You look as though you need a drink. Would a whisky help?'

'*Anything* would help.' Hawthorne squinted suspiciously up at Eric. 'But will I be drinking alone?'

'I'll take an orange juice.'

'And I'll feel vaguely guilty.'

'And more relaxed.' Eric walked across to the cupboard

and poured the drinks for himself and Hawthorne. 'So what's been the problem today?'

Hawthorne took the drink, sipped at it reflectively. 'Glenfiddich. You know how to look after people. Problem? Ahh, the general one, I suppose. Circulars from the Centre saying we have to instigate procedures to crack down on job-dodgers. Job-dodgers! Where the hell's the jobs to dodge? And then there's the real frustration . . . I mean, before 1974 there was a statutory forty-eight per cent ceiling for annual interest. The '74 Act cut that out—to bring in *flexibility*. But it was at least *some* safeguard against extortion. Now, the safeguard is supposed to be that the Act gives people the right to challenge the terms of a loan through the courts. But can I get any of my clients who are hooked on the debts to start a county court action? Can I hell! I've had three people in today, and I just can't get them to move.'

Eric hesitated. 'I think we might have a chink of light at the end of your tunnel.'

'You've got someone who'll stand up in court against Sam Turriff?'

'I think so. It's a bit . . . delicate, and I don't want to push the issue, not yet.'

'Who is it?' Hawthorne asked curiously.

'Tony Cullen.'

Hawthorne sipped his whisky reflectively, then nodded. 'That's the lad whose daughter's disappeared.'

'That's why the time is hardly opportune to ask him to take proceedings against Turriff. The fact is, I'm acting for him in the matter of the kidnapping—though God knows with a marked lack of success so far—and he's intimated that in return he's prepared to do what we want and lay a complaint against Turriff.'

Hawthorne bared his teeth in a grimace of satisfaction. 'If only I can get that bastard into court . . .'

'But we can't use Cullen yet. Not in present circumstances.'

'I see that. I can wait. Anyway, you have something else for me?'

'A few names, and a few questions.' Eric handed the civil servant a sheet of paper. 'I've had Jackie Parton asking around. He's come up with these. They're runners for Turriff. You can add them to your own list. Maybe there'll be contracts you can pick up from them, so we don't need to use Cullen eventually.'

Hawthorne shrugged and scratched his heavy jaw. 'Possible. But only that. Fine, I'll add the names. What about the questions?'

'Have you heard anything about, or from, Heckles?'

Hawthorne frowned. 'That's the young addict you hauled out from under Mason, isn't it? He's on our books, but I don't keep track of everybody, and I haven't had his case brought to my attention. What's your interest in him?'

Eric shrugged. 'I've just had another brush with Detective-Superintendent Mason. He's not a man to give up on grudges. He's got one as far as I'm concerned, and Heckles is certainly a target for him. Anyway, if you do pick up any information on Heckles—particularly if he's been hauled into court again—let me know. I wouldn't want Mason to get his fists on the man.'

'You're building your clientele on inadequates, Eric.'

Eric smiled. 'Everyone seems to be telling me that these days.' He sipped at his orange juice. 'Anyway, the other thing I wanted to ask you is whether you can tell me anything about Ferdy Newton.'

'Newton? He's on the list—one of Sam Turriff's runners. What's your interest in him?'

'I'd like to find out what *his* interest is in *me*.'

'You've had contact with him?'

'Of a threatening nature. I got the impression he was less than pleased I was seeking information about the ticketmen.'

'Well, he wouldn't be happy, would he?' Hawthorne said, grinning. 'Still, what can I tell you about him . . . No great shakes even as a villain. Comes from a large Byker family; about eight kids, as I recall, and they got moved into the Wall some ten years ago when the houses were getting pulled down towards Wallsend. His father, Lyall Newton, didn't keep his activity sexually confined to his wife: he was a notorious womanizer with a burglarious reputation.'

'I saw little lovable in the son.'

Hawthorne laughed. 'Oh, I don't think the old man was anything to write home about as far as looks were concerned. But he got around. Fathered more than a few bastards, the gossip says, and Ferdy will have more than his share of half-brothers and -sisters around the east terraces. But you say he threatened you?'

'Bit vague. He'd got wind of the fact that I'd set Jackie Parton on to investigating the ticket-men and their activities. He warned me off. But he seemed . . . *particularly* angry about my intervention. I got the impression there was more to it than just pressure on his livelihood. Anyway, he warned me, told me I was fishing in deep waters.'

Hawthorne frowned thoughtfully into his whisky glass. 'Mmmm. His old man disappeared, of course. There was some story about a fight down at Pandon, and someone was stabbed. Lyall Newton certainly had a temper, and was not averse to violence. Never heard that Ferdy followed his father in that respect. But the old man disappeared after that killing. Never came back. Ferdy took over really, as head of the household.'

'He took the responsibilities seriously?'

'That's right. A small man in so many ways, but while the family was growing up he hung around, kept things together. You can say that about so many of these petty crooks around the river that they'd sell their own grandmothers. Not Ferdy. Till his mother died he kept pretty close, looked after things. Shows not everyone's completely bad. Mind you, the family lived in something akin to a rookery. Swindlers all.'

'And after his mother died?'

'The family split up. There was a younger brother who went on the rigs, I recall, and there was his sister, Eileen Flannery. Remember her?'

'Don't think so.'

'Ah, she did a bit of singing around the working men's clubs and then got talent-spotted, had a short series on radio and a couple of appearances on television. Career sort of faded once she moved south, but you must remember her . . . bonny lass. Of course, she was the black sheep in a sense, either that or she got too uppity for the family.'

'How do you mean, black sheep? In *that* family?'

Hawthorne grinned. 'She made good for a while in a *legitimate* activity. The Newtons found that a bit hard to live with in their neighbourhood. No, Eileen Flannery—was that her stage name or was *she* one of the half-sisters? She never came back north and it was no loss as far as Ferdy was concerned. He'd look after his ilk, maybe even fiercely —but she could get lost. She wasn't his kind.' He squinted up at Eric. 'What I will say is, watch him. He *is* small but he can be vicious. So go canny.'

'I don't anticipate trouble. Anyway, have you got anything new on Turriff's activities?'

'Not a lot. I've got the dossier prepared against the time someone like Cullen stands up and does his thing. But we still need more information about methods, evidence of direct soliciting—'

'I have a feeling Cullen will come through on that one.'

'—and possession of welfare payment books,' Hawthorne continued. 'Until then . . .'

'I still hope that Jackie Parton will come up with the information we need.'

Hawthorne finished his whisky with a flourish. 'So we wait. Thanks for the whisky. You know, I feel better already.'

Jackie Parton was prepared to use telephones but unwilling to say very much over them. Consequently, when the little ex-jockey phoned in shortly before five o'clock Eric readily agreed to meet him at the foot of Pudding Chare in a few minutes' time. His head was beginning to ache in any case, in the confines of the office poring over taxation papers, and a stroll along the quayside would clear his head of the ache and the prickling of the sensitive nerve-ends behind his eyes.

He saw Parton coming down Dog Leap Stairs and waited at the chare until the little man raised his hand and grinned, apologizing for being a little late. They turned and began to walk away from the shadow of the Tyne Bridge. Down river a tug hooted, warning the traffic of its intention to proceed beyond the bar, to escort the Norwegian ferry into the swing of the river. A Customs launch was boiling stern water, slipping moorings to follow the tug, and gulls squalled above the riggings of a fishing-boat eager to escape the repair yards and return to Tynemouth and the open sea.

'I've just had Nick Hawthorne in to see me,' Eric said. 'Anything more on Turriff?'

Jackie Parton shook his head. 'Doors are closing. I was getting names, as you know, Mr Ward, from the pubs and clubs. The word's out now, though, and people don't want to know. I think Turriff's getting hard-nosed—or his ticket-men are. It wasn't that I wanted to talk to you about, anyway.'

'Cullen?'

'His kid, yeh.' Parton screwed his narrow features up towards the bright sky, blinking at the wheeling greybacks. 'I talked to that Mrs Chaddha, and then made some inquiries about this girl Davinia. Wasn't all that difficult, and I found her eventually in a pad with a sad twenty-year-old called Danny who looks like a wrinkled old monkey. He can't have long ahead of him. You ever seen this stuff, Mr Ward?'

He extended his hand, gnarled fingers opening. Eric saw a few strips of scorched tinfoil and burned matches. He glanced at Parton in surprise. 'Are they important?'

'It's the only kind of evidence you can get, I suppose. Funny, I seen enough of this stuff in the lifts of the tower blocks this last year or so, but never knew what it signified. I mean, I ain't into the drug scene, it's kids, and my contacts are older and certainly not involved with this kind of rubbish.'

'So what's it mean?' Eric asked, aware of an undercurrent of disgust and frustration in the little man.

'Hah, there's this myth among the kids that if they inhale the burned skag it isn't going to hurt them. Chasing the dragon, they call it, and it avoids dirty needles and bad addiction. They're kidding themselves, of course: once they find they're unsatisfied with inhaling, they'll turn to the needle all right. But Mr Ward, they're just *kids*, you knaa? And that's worse, it's kids dealing with kids. It's not like it could be stamped out by nailing a Mister Big somewhere: the estates in the West End, and scattered through Denton and Byker, they're saddled with peddlers who are still in their teens. And I mean young teens. The bloody polis—'

'Jackie,' Eric interrupted, 'they've got their problems too. Most dealers on the streets carry no more than about £500 worth—the size of a lump of sugar. That's difficult enough to control. If you're suggesting the kids themselves have got to be taken—'

'All I can say, Mr Ward, is that things have changed,' the ex-jockey insisted stubbornly. 'When I grew up in the West End there was plenty of crime, but it wasna like this. I tell you, this . . . is *hopeless*, man!'

'So what's happened?' Eric asked quietly.

The ex-jockey slowed, turned, walked towards the guard rail and leaned on it, staring down into the black waters below him. He opened his hand, let the foil and the matches fall, and watched the glint of the scorched foil as it bobbed away on the current. 'I followed the leads, I came across this kid—not a bad-looking youngster but heading bad, believe me. This Danny character was very high; he tried to stop me talking to her but one push and he collapsed in a corner. I didn't like that, Mr Ward. And I didn't like talking to her.'

'She was there when Kate Cullen was kidnapped?'

'She saw it. I questioned her, and it wasn't easy. She wouldn't concentrate, kept drifting around in her mind, smiling sometimes, content. She reached out for me, Mr Ward, tried to get me to use her—dammit, I'm old enough to be her father, and older!'

'Go on,' Eric said grimly.

'It's dirty work, Mr Ward, and I'm not happy about it.'

Eric could understand the revulsion, and the hint of rebellion also. Parton had been asked to do an investigative job and he had done it, but the circumstances had soured him, raised the bile in his throat. He felt resentful, and if his anger was vague and undirected it could be turned against himself. It was what was happening.

Eric Ward took a deep breath. 'Jackie, listen to me. I ask you from time to time to do a job for me. There's no compulsion. Equally, there's no compulsion for me to do my job. You know my wife's a rich woman; you know I could work for Morcomb Estates; you know I don't *need* to work down here on the Quayside. So why do I do it? Not because it's glamorous. The law isn't glamorous, not the lower reaches, anyway. Court work is all about people's mistakes and weaknesses and sadnesses. I don't see myself as a Galahad; I don't see myself as saving people from themselves, or the consequences of their own folly. Most of my work is dirty, small and unpleasant. But *sometimes* I have cases where someone *innocent* needs help. A child has been kidnapped, Jackie. That's bad in anybody's book. And what you're doing—unpleasant though it may be—is necessary, if we are to find Tony Cullen's daughter.'

Jackie Parton shrugged and stared at his broken-knuckled hands. 'I know it,' he half-whispered, 'but even so . . . Aye, you're right. I know it. This kid, dammit she's little better than a whore already and on the habit as well; she got to tell me eventually. She saw the snatch; she saw the car; she saw the men inside.'

'She can identify them?'

'She's not sure about the driver. But she had approached them a few days earlier, tried to get them to pick her up.'

'They were watching the school?'

'Checking times and movements, is my guess. Finding out how long they'd normally have to grab the kid before Mrs Chaddha arrived to collect her.'

'And she thinks she would recognize the passenger in the car?'

A seagull mewed plaintively above their heads. Jackie nodded reflectively. 'He gave her a rough time, it seems. She'd recognize him again. Better than that, she can tell us who he is.'

'She *knows* him?'

'That's right. He's called Lister. Eddie Lister. A big man with a scar on his nose.'

The unnaturally bright fields of rape were like yellow scars along the rising hills, glistening in the late afternoon sunlight as Eric drove north from Newcastle to Sedleigh Hall. A sullen thundercloud menaced Coquetdale, darkening the river, but the Cheviots were sharp and clear against a bright sky and Eric drove carefully, not hurrying, savouring the evening and the rolling hills and the peacefulness of the quiet winding road once he had left the A1.

Eddie Lister.

The name was not known to Jackie Parton, but the ex-jockey had little doubt that he would be able to trace the man by some judicious questioning in the West End. Scotswood did not forget its sons nor turn its back on them and Parton was well-known: Davinia knew Lister so he must have some connection with the north bank. Parton was confident. He would be getting in touch quickly, he hoped, and then perhaps it would be time to call in the police. Not before. Eric Ward did not want Detective-Superintendent

Mason muddying waters before time: if there *was* any sort
of cover-up for Liam Geraghty, Eric wanted to give Mason
and his ilk the minimum time and opportunity to swing it
into action.

The rhododendrons had faded in the long driveway but
the copper beech was magnificent, the ornamental lake thick
with water-lilies, and the bell tower encrusted with dark
green ivy.

In front of the Hall itself, parked in the circular driveway,
was a Rolls-Royce, white, with a distinctive registration
mark. Eric recognized it and something inside him was cold.
He parked his own car near the stables, and walked around
to the terrace at the back of the hall. They were there, with
drinks: Anne looking cool, elegant and welcoming in a
shantung silk dress, Liam Geraghty in open-necked shirt,
cavalry twill trousers, highly polished brown shoes. His eyes
were confident as he watched Eric approach, but his body
was tense as he rose with Anne to greet Eric.

Anne kissed Eric lightly on the cheek, took his arm, and
he could feel tension in her fingers too. 'A drink, darling?'

'I feel I need one. A small Scotch, please, Anne.'

Geraghty waved his glass negligently. 'The odd one
doesn't do any harm.'

'I'm surprised to see you here, Geraghty,' Eric said
calmly. Behind him he heard the chink of ice in the glass.

'I was in the vicinity. Had a chat with that young lawyer
of Anne's, Mark Fenham. Sharp. I'm not sure I can put one
over on him. So I thought I'd come out, explain to your
wife.'

'That you're unlikely to do business with Morcomb Estates after all?'

Liam Geraghty had been about to sip his whisky. The
movement of his arm was arrested, almost imperceptibly,
but the hesitation was there. He sipped, his eyes watching
Eric, and then he nodded thoughtfully. 'Something like that.
You . . . er . . . don't seem surprised.'

'I'm not.'

'Well, I was,' Anne remarked firmly as she joined them, offering Eric the glass. 'I thought the negotiations were well on the way. Mark had told me—'

'I don't think Mr Geraghty was ever particularly interested in the land,' Eric said. 'The likelihood of a deal was always remote.'

Geraghty laughed, a short barking sound. 'You're wrong there, Ward. Your attitude explains to me why indeed you haven't joined Morcomb Estates to help your wife. Business plans change, new priorities arise, shareholdings differ in value as market shifts occur. I was explaining to Mrs Ward—'

'Save me the explanation. I've had time to think, Geraghty. The deal was never on.'

The beefy face of the Irishman began to take on a different colour. He raised his head, his arrogant nose jutting out menacingly. 'You sound very confident. Very sure of yourself.'

'I told you. I've had time to think.'

'And . . .?'

'Things slip into place.'

'What things?'

Eric glanced at Anne standing silently beside him. She was watching him warily, not understanding, but feeling the strained atmosphere between the two men, aware of the hostility that lay curbed beneath the surface politeness, a veneer already cracking with the edges of sharpness in their tones. He smiled at her, coolly, but reassuringly. 'A number of things. There was a conversation I walked into, between Anne and Mark Fenham. They were discussing your motives in setting up negotiations with Morcomb Estates. I thought they were wrong; I thought there were other reasons. I told you, on the fell.'

'I remember,' Geraghty said coldly.

'But *I* was wrong too, wasn't I? I was still thinking along business tracks. But it was never about business at all.'

'I don't understand,' Anne said in a tight little voice.

'There was something else that bothered me at the time,' Eric continued, 'but I couldn't understand what it was that was making me uneasy. Mr Geraghty here, he can act like the original stage Irishman at times: tell jokes, charm birds from trees, *use* his background to get what he wants. If he was *really* interested in setting up a deal with Morcomb Estates he would surely have found it necessary to be, at the least, affable towards me—the husband of the owner of the company. Quite the reverse: on the fell, he was actually unpleasant.'

Anne glanced at Geraghty, unsure. 'In what way?'

'That doesn't matter,' Eric said quickly, and a flicker of malice touched Liam Geraghty's fleshy mouth. 'The point is, why did he behave like that? I've thought about it; now I think I know why. He simply didn't *care*.'

'Care about the negotiations?' Anne asked.

'About the negotiations, certainly, because they weren't serious. But not about his surroundings, either. The people he was with. The morning; the shoot. None of it. His mind was elsewhere.'

'Eric, you're talking in riddles!'

'He's talking *rubbish*, Mrs Ward.' But Geraghty's glance was still watchful and he was still listening.

'The fact is, Anne, he didn't care, he wasn't bothered even to be pleasant because he had no interest in what was happening about him. He was *waiting* for something, and the tension of that wait came out in the way he behaved. It isn't characteristic of Mr Geraghty to be boorish in business company, of that I'm sure, but it seems he loses a little control when he's worried, or maybe scared.'

'*Scared?*' Geraghty scoffed at the thought. 'What did I have to be scared of?'

'That events on the south bank of the Tyne might not have gone as planned the previous afternoon.'

The silence between the three of them lengthened as the big Irishman stared at the golden liquid in his glass. Across the meadow, among the tall trees, a family of rooks rose in a black cloud, cawing complaint at the disturbance of a tractor in the field; on the purpling hills rising to the Cheviot the late sun was warm and gentle. Geraghty cleared his throat and looked up at Eric under beetling brows. 'We need to talk, Mr Ward.'

'We are talking.'

'I detect an edge of belligerence in your tone. I'm not used to having lawyers speak to me that way.'

'I'm indifferent to what you're used to, Geraghty. I certainly resent my family and my home being used by a man such as you, for such a purpose.'

Anne stared at him in surprise. *'Used?'*

'Geraghty used Morcomb Estates and used our hospitality; the one to have a good reason to be in England, close to the scene of operations at the important time, and the other to have a solid alibi—no presence, no contact, no knowledge of events—when the crime was committed.'

'Crime?'

Anne's bewilderment was not matched in Geraghty's purring tone as he repeated the word. 'Crime . . . a harsh word, Ward. And you talk of home and family. What about my home, my family?'

'You've never made a home. You rarely saw your granddaughter. You had had little contact with your *daughter* over the years.'

'I don't need to take this,' Geraghty rumbled menacingly.

'I didn't ask you here.'

For a moment Eric thought the big man was about to lose his temper. A fist clenched, colour grew high in the man's face, but he controlled himself, finished his whisky and set the glass down. 'I'm not here to defend my lifestyle or that of my daughter. I just want to make sure you understand a few things.'

'I understand all I need to. And I hope to prove that you were involved in the snatching of your granddaughter from the father who holds the right to her custody!'

'You don't know what the hell you're talking about,'

Geraghty sneered. 'You can't bluff me—'

'I know you've put on pressure—you've been in touch with the Lord Lieutenant, you've had conversations with the Chief Constable. You persuaded them that the kidnapping could leave your granddaughter's life in danger, that they need to play it down, wait for the ransom demand, a matter of days. But when it comes out do you think they won't be running for cover? You've connived at your own daughter's snatching of Kate—and God knows what effect that violence will have on the child! But you don't really give a damn, just as long as you and your daughter get back your *possessions*! But if I track down the man who carried out that kidnapping you'll find yourself inside with him and the *notables* in this county will hardly be your friends then! You'll end up in prison, Geraghty, and your bloody money won't save you then!'

'Are you finished?' Geraghty was still controlling his temper, but with difficulty. He glared at Eric furiously, and his mouth was like iron. But though his tone was bitter, it was level, tight. 'What the hell do you know about any of it? I deny absolutely what you're saying—you'll never prove I had a hand in Kate's kidnapping. All that's happened is that you've been listening to the obsessed ravings of a piece of Gateshead scum that was never anything but garbage and never will be! Haven't you got the picture yet? The things he told you—can you really believe them? I *love* my daughter. I indulged her, gave her everything she needed. I went along with it when she decided to strike out on her own, even coming north to this godforsaken county! But my worst fears were realized. She wanted to kick over a few traces but that bum Cullen took advantage of her. She didn't know much, she'd had a protected life in Ireland, and he seduced her, got her pregnant, fed her a load of romantic hogwash about living in a rose-ridden cottage! And then what? He loses his job, can't support her, refuses to work for me, accepts my charity when it suits him and when Ruth decides to come to her senses, pick up the career she started, he calls her a whore! I tell you, Ward, when she made a success of her life, moved into the business world, showed that she was *my* daughter, it was the worst pill he had to swallow. She was a success; he would always be a failure!'

'And what about Kate?' Eric snapped back, stemming the tirade. 'What about the daughter she abandoned?'

'*Abandoned?* What the hell choice did she have? She had to express her personality—other men stay home and look after the kid in similar situations where the woman can be the breadwinner! But it stuck in his gullet; his northern pride couldn't accept that, and he threw her out, barred the door to her, effectively! What's better—to stay away or fight a tug-of-war over the child?'

'Isn't that what happened anyway? A return, an upsetting of the girl, a court hearing, and after a defeat, a kidnapping of the child? Hell's flames, man, can you hear yourself?'

'Eric—' Anne was touching his arm, warningly. He was going too far, overreacting, becoming emotionally involved and the prickling behind his eyes told him the tensions were getting to him, raising his demand for an easing drug.

'Can I hear *myself?*' Geraghty rasped. 'What about you? Why are you taking this so personally? You see yourself as some kind of white knight riding to rescue that bastard Cullen and his claims on my granddaughter? Look at the reality of the situation, for one moment. What the hell will Cullen ever give the child but hopelessness? He can't support her, he has to borrow money. He can't look after her properly, he keeps her in a squalid slum—'

'It seems to me you could have helped more positively there,' Eric interrupted. 'Neither you nor your daughter broke your backs to do anything for the child.'

'What the hell is *that* supposed to mean?'

Eric shook his head angrily. 'Cullen told me that he got a court order—'

'Which was never bloody well necessary!'

'He got a court order for maintenance of Kate, but although payments were made initially, once Ruth was back in the States for a while the payments dried up, and Cullen was left to fend for his daughter—your granddaughter—for himself.'

'That's a bloody lie!' Geraghty's eyes glittered fiercely as he glared at Eric. 'That little bastard Cullen doesn't know the truth when he sees it. The court order he got, that was just malice on his part. I'd have given him the money . . . I *had* been giving him money. The fact was, his pride wouldn't let him accept it in the end. And even the court order, it was a way of getting at Ruth, and when she pays it, what does he do? He drops out!'

'That's a fanciful excuse—'

'I tell you, the address we had for Cullen kept changing, and in the end we just lost trace of him and the cheques came back with no forwarding address. What was Ruth supposed to do, set a private detective on him, get the police to *force* him to take the money?' Geraghty snorted in contempt. 'I tell you, he kept moving, getting into slummier addresses, and all the while the kid had nothing to look forward to, not even the love and affection of her mother! If he had stayed put, he'd have got the money. As it was, I had a hell of a job tracing him—'

'So you could kidnap Kate?' Eric asked softly.

For a moment Geraghty's features went rigid, his mouth stiff as iron, a shadow flickering over his eyes. Then he uttered an obscenity. 'Ward, I deny any involvement in the kidnapping of my granddaughter. Damn it, there's not even any proof yet that there's been a snatch! You can't trap me with cracks like that—and you're getting stuck into stuff that could break your back! I came here to reason with you, suggest you back off quietly, drop Cullen, stop listening to his lies, even do some lucrative work for me in its stead. But you can forget that now. You're a crazy bastard who's heading for a cliff and I'm not about to try to stop you. What I *am* saying is this: you keep pushing against me and someone could get killed. Lay off; stay away from me, my business and my family, and get back to your bloody inadequates on the Quayside. I'm dealing in realities, not romance.'

'You're dealing in illegality and violence!'

'The reality is Kate will be better off with her mother,' Geraghty almost shouted, 'and that's all I got to say about it. And I warn you again: back off, or there could be blood over all sorts of carpets!'

He needed the atropine for the first time in a long while. The whisky hadn't helped; anger, alcohol and his irritation at finding Geraghty in his home had tipped the balance. When the man had stormed from the hall Anne had been strangely subdued. Eric had been disinclined to talk further of the matter so her silence had been welcome to that extent. On the other hand it also suggested that perhaps in something he was wrong. The thought twisted in his mind, forcing him to go over the story Cullen had told him, hearing again Geraghty's impassioned, angry tones. Where did the truth ever lie in personal relationships? In conflict, with wild words flying between man and wife and with a scared child in between, what ever was justifiable?

As the sensitivity behind his eyes gentled he thought about what was driving him. A sense of justice: it was as simple as that. Geraghty's arguments held a degree of logic, but logic was not law.

And yet what was it that damned ophthalmic surgeon had said to him about those who had faced blindness and had been pulled back from the brink? *It's not that they don't accept reality . . . rather, their sense of reality is blurred.*

Geraghty claimed to be the realist in this matter. Eric Ward clung to law, and justice. Did that constitute a blurred reality?

4

Jackie Parton waited.

A fine mist lay along the river banks, a sea fret that had ghosted in late that afternoon against the echo of distant ship sirens from Tynemouth, eight miles away. The mist dampened the city sounds so that on the hillside he had the impression it was a Sunday, the town sleeping off the carousals of the city centre on Saturday night.

He waited and still the prickling feeling along his back suggested to him that this was a mistake. Something was wrong, something out of phase. He glanced at his watch: Eric Ward should be along in a little while as they'd arranged, to be picked up at the station on the Carlisle line. Jackie frowned and thought back to a crowded two days.

It was ironic, of course, that it had been at The Hydraulic Engine he had found the answers. He'd tramped the city, talked to people in the pubs, out at the racecourse, down on the Quayside. He'd worked the market and the night-clubs, talked to squatters in Denton and vagrants in Pandon. At four in the morning he'd had to explain himself to an unfriendly copper in a Panda car and at five to a disbelieving widow with whom he'd been living for the last six months. Neither had entirely accepted his explanations; both had turned their backs eventually and stopped their questioning.

But it was at lunch-time, when he'd more or less given up and decided to have a refresher in his own local, that Jackie had heard what he wanted to hear. The informant was an old acquaintance, a heavy, pot-bellied man with grizzled eyebrows, little hair and a sagging, defeated face. He had played for Newcastle Reserves as a young man, when Jackie Milburn was firing the terraces with his sharpshooting. That was a long time ago. He still clung to the name 'Goalie' Edwards as a reminder of past glories that might have been, but the years had left him with a rime of suspicion about his mouth.

'Glass o' broon? Aye, I could take that, Jackie.'

When Jackie had returned to the table in the dark corner of the pub Goalie Edwards had sipped the beer reflectively, then squinted across to the ex-jockey. 'So, what's all this I hear aboot you askin' questions along the river, hey? You wanta watch yoursel', Jackie.'

'I can take care of myself.'

'Not with heavies, you canna. That business down at Gateshead, now; you don't wanta get messed aboot with that. All very well for the polis to start runnin' around screaming: they get paid to do that. But you stay away from this skag scene, laddie. Dangerous.'

'I don't know what you're talking about, Goalie.'

'You been askin' after Eddie Lister, haven't you?'

'Not in connection with drugs.'

Goalie Edwards had scowled thoughtfully into his beer. 'Is that so? I hear he gets into all sorts of heavy stuff, but what with that chap lifting the skag from that safe house, and the coppers runnin' around fit to bust, I thought . . . So what you want Lister for, then?'

'You know him?'

'Why aye.'

'And how I can reach him?'

'If I knew what you wanted to talk to him about.'

Jackie had hesitated for a while before he spoke. Men like Goalie Edwards could have tough exteriors but could be touched; their loyalties on the other hand were strong, and there was the chance Goalie would still say nothing, if Jackie prevaricated. He had taken the decision. 'You've heard about the kidnapping of that young girl?'

Goalie's eyes had widened. 'The Cullen kid? Why aye, I heard she got snatched. Are you saying . . .'

'My information is Lister was involved. I want to talk to him.'

'With the polis?'

Jackie Parton knew better than that. 'No. I'm working with a solicitor. Just want to contact Lister, have a chat with him, find out who's behind the kidnapping. He'll talk; he'll have a lot to lose.'

'The bastard. Never did like him; loud-mouthed, hard, bit of a psycho, you knaa? And he was in on that snatch?' Goalie Edwards lumbered to his feet. 'Lemme get you a drink, Jackie.'

He had remained reluctant to end the conversation, tell Jackie how he could get in touch with Lister. He had waxed angry about football hooliganism on the modern terraces, about the way the gangs along the river seemed to get away with violence with impunity, and he had argued at length that the only remedy was vigilantism. 'Gotta do wor own thing, Jackie. Eye for an eye, that sort of thing. No good goin' to the polis, or them soft judges. If any bastard touched one of my family, I'd have his guts.'

Goalie Edwards was unmarried and, as far as Jackie knew, without family. But as the afternoon advanced and it grew near closing time Edwards became even more effusive as the beer fuddled his brain. 'Thass the only way, Jackie. Kick the buggers back. Do it to them, like they done it to you. I feel sorry for that Cullen lad. Know him, a bit; seen him around. His mam used to live up in Cullercoats, you knaa. He didn't deserve to get his kid snatched by a bastard like Lister . . .'

It was three o'clock before Goalie Edwards finally gave Jackie the information he required. At three-thirty Jackie learned that Eric Ward would not be back in the office until five. At four-thirty the bronze Scirocco, with Eddie Lister at the wheel, pulled out of Edgecumbe Road and drove west.

It was seven o'clock before Eric Ward arrived at the station.

Jackie explained, as he hurriedly drove through the narrow streets and headed for the south shore.

'I thought it best to go to the address Goalie Edwards

gave me. I hadn't been there half an hour before Lister arrived, in a bronze VW. I tried to contact you but you were in court. I waited, then about four-thirty Lister left his place and drove west, crossed the Redheugh Bridge and went to that scruffy area down by the staiths.'

There had been another car in the area, one that was vaguely familiar. It had picked up the bronze Scirocco, certainly not a great distance from Edgecumbe Road. It had bothered Jackie, made his task of trailing Lister more difficult.

'At times it was like a bloody procession. Anyway, in the end I parked and did the last bit on foot. There's only one road out of that estate. I found the Scirocco parked on some waste ground. Couldn't be seen from the main road. And the other car—a Morris—it was in the next street. I waited, but nothing seemed to be happening. I phoned in again, arranged to pick you up, but having to come to fetch you means we might have missed the bastard.'

Eric Ward said nothing. They drove down the bank and into the estate. The sea fret blanked out the upper storeys of the blocks of flats. The area was like fifty others in the North-East but dirtier, decrepit, run-down, a legacy of mindless building in the Fifties, crumbling into decay now and largely uninhabited, a ghost town for the homeless and the drifting. The Scirocco was still there.

'Where's the other car parked?' Ward asked.

Jackie showed him the place. The car had gone.

'So what do we do now?' Jackie asked.

'Watch the Scirocco. When Lister gets back to it, we'll have a little chat.'

They parked some distance away, where they could maintain a watch upon the car parked on the wasteland. An hour went by and the darkness gathered greyly and wetly about them.

At eight-thirty the first of the police cars entered the estate, noisily, and with blue light flashing. Two others arrived within twenty minutes. At that point, with the

Scirocco still unattended, Eric decided they should leave. Jackie nosed his car out towards the main road.

The police car waved them down. The constable was polite, but firm. He asked for their names; he used his walkie-talkie. Then he gestured for them to pull in to the side.

Ten minutes later a detective-superintendent in plain clothes approached the car. He stood at the passenger door, stared grimly in at Eric. 'What the hell are you doing here?'

'I might ask the same of you, Mason,' Eric replied.

'Don't play silly buggers with me, I'm on business here! What's *your* business in this midden?'

Eric hesitated, glanced at Jackie, and decided there was nothing served by a refusal to explain. Mason would have them both down at headquarters with an obstruction charge: the man was obviously in the mood for it.

'I want to interview a man called Lister. He drove here; we followed him. With all this activity—'

'*Get out.*'

Mason opened the door and Eric got out, Jackie Parton following reluctantly. The burly detective glared at them both for a moment, an odd glint of malicious satisfaction in his eyes and then turned abruptly, waving to them to follow him.

They crossed a littered yard, entered a crumbling building in which damp had peeled long strips of plaster from the walls and vandals had smashed everything capable of being broken. A black cat glared at them from the darkness of the stairwell, poised to flee. Mason ignored it, and clumped his way up to the first storey. A litter of empty bottles and the smell of methylated spirits greeted them in the small room. It opened out into two larger rooms and what had once passed for a bathroom.

Two police constables made way for them to pass through and into the next corridor. Doors had been removed to allow a rookery of passageways for the vagrants who used these buildings. Mason stopped, half turned and pointed. Lying against the wall was a dark, crumpled shape.

He was lying huddled, a big, heavy man clasping his stomach, bent over in agony. The life, drawn out of him by the knife, would have left him slowly and painfully. Outside in the street a siren approached, wailing through the sea fret. The forensic unit was on its way. Mason bared his teeth unpleasantly.

'Eddie Lister, you said? You wanted to interview him? You won't find it easy now, Ward! But be my guest!'

His laughter had a macabre, malicious tone that was echoed from the dark stairwell below their feet.

CHAPTER 4

1

'So what on earth happened?'

The early gold of the morning sky had given way to a warm flush spreading above the hills to the west. The sunlight tipped the ridge, bringing it to green life while the hollows of the valley below remained purple, the colour fading reluctantly against the invasion of the morning. Unshaven, haggard from the long night, Eric sipped the welcoming coffee and gazed about him while Anne waited in her dressing-gown for a reply.

When the sun glinted on the river across the meadows Eric finished his coffee, turned and managed a smile. 'I'm sorry. I need to wind down for a few minutes. You got the phone call?'

'Only to say you were at police headquarters at Morpeth. It wasn't very explicit. I assumed at first you were there with a client.'

'Not quite like that, I'm afraid.' Eric stretched, and looked at his watch. 'I can't say it wasn't an eye-opening experience, being on the other side of the fence, so to speak. I've done enough interrogating in my time, and I've seen enough villains in the police cells. It's an odd experience, being taken for one.'

'So what *happened?*'

Eric held out a hand to take hers. She looked very young this morning; there was a defencelessness about her that brought an ache to his throat. It was odd how it could strike him on occasions, when he'd been so reluctant to marry her, the thought that without her now he would be lost. Perhaps that was why he had avoided the commitment, because it would make him vulnerable. Yet now it was she who was looking vulnerable.

'Jackie Parton got information from a young girl called Davinia. She was able to identify one of the men who had kidnapped Kate Cullen. His name was Eddie Lister. It took Jackie two days to trace Lister: he found him at a Newcastle address, got in touch with me, and then followed Lister when he left home and drove to the West End, and then Gateshead.'

'Where was he going, or why?'

Eric shook his head. 'That's a question the police got around to asking us, but we've no answers. You see, it's fairly clear he was going to the flats above the staiths to meet someone but we don't know who.' Eric paused. 'I've got a feeling Jackie knows something else which he hasn't even told me, something about who Lister was due to meet, but I'm not sure. Anyway, he came to pick me up, we drove back to the staiths, and then waited for Lister to return to his car. There was no way we could know which building he'd entered. Then the police came.'

Anne walked across to the terrace wall and stood with her back to it. The red-gold tints in her hair were highlighted in the soft morning sun. 'The police just *happened* to come along?'

. 'No, that couldn't be it. A patrol car, obviously, responding to a call, I would guess. Maybe somebody in the flats had heard a struggle and called in. I don't know. Anyway, the first car must have radioed in, and then Mason—'

'*He's* involved?'

'Unfortunately, yes. He was not displeased to see me there. They arrived, found Lister, and then found me and Jackie. We had some explaining to do, and we had to do it at Morpeth.'

'And Lister?'

'Knifed. Nasty.'

'But why?'

Eric yawned. 'That's the question. Look, do you mind if I get to bed? I'm almost falling apart.'

She lay beside him in the soft light. He told her, in a drowsy voice, of the verbal battering Mason had given them, and of the persistent questioning to which they had been individually subjected. It had been no time to stand on rights, to raise legal technicalities. He had tried to cooperate, knowing that if Mason could get any mud to stick it could mean the end of Eric Ward's legal career. But he had been able to provide very little information that was of any consequence. He had repeated, time and again, that he had never met Lister, had wanted to talk to him about the kidnapping, and never had the chance to do so. His story had tied in with Jackie Parton's.

Anne's fingers were cool on his forehead and his eyes were heavy. In spite of his weariness, he was aware of the silkiness of her skin and in a little while he turned, to lie closer to her. Her touch lingered on his mouth, and then moved to recognize the responses of his body. In a little while, softly and gently, they explored each other and made love, and the morning slipped away in drowsy, relieved sensation.

Later, when the sun was slanting in brightly through the windows and Anne had brought him some breakfast of rolls and orange juice, she asked him who he thought Lister had gone to meet.

'If I knew that, I might know who killed him.'

'But who do you *think*?'

Eric looked at her quizzically. 'You were rather taken with Liam Geraghty, weren't you?'

'I wouldn't say that.' She grinned self-consciously. 'He's a very . . . positive person. There's a strength—a very *male* strength about him. I don't know . . . what he had to say to you had a ring about it. I know it doesn't match what Tony Cullen had to say about his relationship with Ruth Geraghty, but at the same time . . . On the other hand, maybe I find him attractive because I like older men!'

'Ouch!' Eric said, and smiled.

Anne herself sobered. She stared at him, weighing something in her mind. 'Why are we talking about Liam Geraghty?'

'To get you off an unpleasant subject.'

'Or because you think it was he who had a rendezvous at the staiths with this man Lister.'

'Darling, I really don't know. The fact is, the police were not in the slightest bit interested last night in any theories about a connection between the killing of Eddie Lister and the kidnapping of Kate Cullen. They were quite dismissive of it: they were sure there is no connection.' He finished his orange juice and swung his legs out of bed. 'So what do you make of that?'

'Your legs?'

'The dismissiveness.'

'I'm not sure,' she said slowly. 'But I've always liked your legs.'

He laughed, and began to dress.

'Liam Geraghty,' she said.

'Yes?'

'I'm sure he couldn't have had anything to do with Lister's murder.'

'I'm less certain than you. Look, why are the police so dismissive?'

'I'm not certain I understand.'

'They are so positive there's no connection between the murder and the kidnapping because they're no longer interested in the kidnapping—if they've ever been! It means only one thing: our suspicions have been right from the start and Tony Cullen had it worked out. Ruth Geraghty wanted her daughter back, and Liam Geraghty set it up.'

'But where could Kate be now?'

Eric chose a fresh shirt and slipped it on. 'My guess is she's on her way to the States already, if she hasn't met her mother in Ireland. You see, it's so easy. Geraghty sets up the kidnapping, spirits the girl safely away to Ireland via Newcastle Airport, or the shuttle from Manchester, and makes sure that the police are persuaded this is a family matter and nothing else. All right, maybe he held them off with the ransom demand in the first instance, but my guess is he'll have come clean by now, and they'll be too embarrassed to do much about it. That, and the donations he's no doubt made to various police charities.'

'You've become cynical.'

'Maybe so.'

'So you think Ruth Geraghty and Kate will be together in Ireland?'

'Or the States. Either way, Geraghty set it up. And that brings us back to Lister. Suppose he got greedy, or nervous?'

'How do you mean?'

'Maybe he thought he wasn't being paid enough. Or maybe he heard that Jackie Parton was asking questions around Tyneside. Perhaps, for one of these reasons, he put pressure on Geraghty. It could be Geraghty arranged to meet him. Not personally, of course: that bloody Irishman would never do his own physical dirty work, of that I'm sure.'

'You mean he could have sent someone to kill Lister?' Anne asked, wide-eyed.

'Not necessarily *kill* him. Maybe persuade him. On occasions like that, however, things can get out of hand.'

'And in a struggle—'

'Lister gets knifed.'

Eric reached into the wardrobe and slipped on a jacket.

He turned to face Anne; she was staring at him soberly. 'Where are you going? You're not letting this go, are you?'

'Anne, I can't. Not now. I'm still acting for Tony Cullen and I'll get his daughter back—or I'll see the bastards who did it in court. That includes Geraghty. It doesn't now include Eddie Lister. But Lister wasn't alone in that car. We know Geraghty wasn't there because he was at Sedleigh with us. I want to find out just who *was* in the car with Lister when Kate was kidnapped.'

'And if you find him?'

'I think I might also have found the man who knifed Eddie Lister.'

When he arrived at his office on the Quayside Eric learned that Lizzie, the punk-styled legal executive who ran an efficient office for him in spite of her appearance, had arranged an appointment for him later that afternoon. 'There were a few people who phoned in,' she explained, 'but I put them off since you hadn't said what time you were likely to be coming in. This one I thought you'd like to keep.'

'Who is it?'

'Mr Cullen.'

She looked at him rather oddly as she spoke and he wondered for a moment whether Lizzie had heard about his interrogation the previous evening at Morpeth. Or maybe she was beginning to know him as all close employees got to know their employers: too well. Maybe she guessed that he was getting closely involved with the Cullen case, and perhaps *too* closely involved. Blurring realities.

He had time to deal with several files and a letter inviting him to undertake work for a shipping company on Tyneside, dealing with freight contracts. It would mean he'd have to brush up on his maritime law, but a stronger commercial practice would be a good thing as far as he was concerned so he replied affirmatively. After that, he had a little while to sit back and think.

His conversation with Anne that morning had helped clear his own thoughts somewhat, and what he had told her certainly matched the facts at his disposal. He still felt he was missing something. Perhaps Tony Cullen would be able to supply some missing threads.

Cullen arrived some ten minutes late. He was dressed in a windbreaker and jeans and he looked like Eric had felt the previous night. Clearly, the loss of his daughter and his failure to find out anything about the circumstances had affected him badly. His curly hair was dishevelled and there was a pallor about his freckled face that Eric had not seen before. His light blue eyes held a haunted, anxious look and he was unshaven. He sat down in the chair Eric offered with a listlessness that was uncharacteristic, and the stubbornness of his mouth seemed to have disappeared. Defeat had marked him, and weariness.

'Are you all right, Cullen?'

Tony Cullen failed to meet his glance. He shrugged, stared at the carpet. 'I come in to talk to you about Sam Turriff. I owe it to you.'

'I don't understand.'

Cullen glanced briefly up to Eric and frowned. 'You been pretty good with me. I shouldn't have reacted the way I did at the beginning. I know since then you been working pretty hard, asking questions and all that. It won't have done you much good with the police. Not helping *me*. And it's my problem: no need for them to get the needle at you. But they will. I know the bastards. Geraghty's got them sewed up, and you'll just get your business knocked about.'

'That's my worry, not yours,' Eric said firmly.

'No. About Turriff. What do you want from me?'

Eric hesitated. 'Well, if you're sure you want to help . . . The fact is, we can nail him in court if we can disclose illegal activity on his part, or by ticket-men acting on his instructions.'

'He's got a system,' Cullen said wearily. 'He worked it with me, certainly, first time I went to him. He claims—

boasts is a better word—that he doesn't act for security. But as the ticket-man explains first time around, while they don't call for security, there is the fact that Turriff's got a lot of cash floating on Tyneside and he's got to be sure he can haul it in. So you hand over to the ticket-man your welfare book. You just sign the forms in advance and the ticket-man holds them. He takes them along, cashes them as they fall due, collects the supplementary benefits or unemployment pay, deducts the money due to Turriff and hands over the rest to the punter. That's how it's done.'

'How did you make contact with Turriff?'

'I didn't. His ticket-men prowl the Job Centre, and they also got manors of their own. They approach you.'

'Are you prepared,' Eric said slowly, 'to make a statement along these lines?'

'Why not?'

'And appear in court, if necessary?'

Cullen hesitated, then shrugged indifferently. 'Okay.'

Eric reached for the phone and called Frances. The young girl arrived a few minutes later, armed with notebook and pencil. For the next twenty minutes she took a shorthand transcript of the conversation between Eric and Cullen as they spoke of systems, times, dates and names. When it was finished Eric told Frances she could leave; the statements could be transcribed the following day.

When the door had closed behind her Eric said to Cullen, 'You look as though you could use a drink.'

'I can that, Mr Ward.'

Eric poured a glass of whisky for him; Cullen seemed not to notice that Eric himself was not drinking. 'You seem troubled,' Eric said.

Tony Cullen nodded. His head was lowered and he stared unseeingly at the glass in his hand. His shoulders were hunched unhappily, his hands uneasy, trembling slightly. He looked as though he had barely slept for days. 'I been thinking, Mr Ward.'

'About what?'

'About Kate.'

'And?'

'Maybe I been wrong.'

'I don't understand.'

Cullen shrugged unhappily. 'Not wrong about her being snatched by Geraghty and Ruth: I'm still convinced that's what happened. But maybe wrong about the way I reacted to it.'

'In what way? I would have said your reaction was completely normal.'

'Maybe so. But who's to say I haven't been wrong all along, trying to keep Kate with me? Mr Ward, I love my kid, but maybe I've been selfish too. It's possible I got mad at the kidnapping not just because I love Kate and was worried, but because I hated to see Ruth and that bastard Geraghty *winning*.'

'Kidnapping,' Eric said slowly, 'is a criminal offence whichever way you look at it.'

'All right, I know that, Mr Ward, but what I'm trying to say is, that apart, what's to be done? You know as well as I do that Kate could well be in Ireland by now, or maybe even on her way to the States. Ruth has got her own money as well as her father's behind her: they could shuttle around over there so much I wouldn't even know where they were. I got no money to chase them. I got no money to pay for expensive lawyers in the States—'

'I think you ought to realize,' Eric interrupted, 'the English courts will take a serious view of what has happened. If we can prove Kate was kidnapped by Ruth Geraghty, mother or not, we can get an extradition order—'

'But that's what I'm really *talking* about,' Cullen protested, his mouth twisting unhappily, marked with uncertainty. 'Would I be doing right in getting one of them extradition orders? I mean, what would Kate be coming back to? A scruffy flat, a father who can't get a job, indifferent schooling; no prospects for her on Tyneside when she grows up because every other person's out of work. Do you see what I mean? In the States there'd be Ruth's business, and Geraghty's financial support if things went wrong in that. All right, they'd be *winning*—'

'Tell me,' Eric said carefully, 'is that why you refused financial support from Ruth Geraghty before? Because by allowing Ruth to support Kate you were losing something?' As Cullen's head came up Eric went on, '*You* told me she had stopped sending you money for Kate. Geraghty tells a different story. Your constant moving caused them to lose trace for a while, and the cheques were returned. You made no attempt to recover that money.'

Cullen shrugged despondently. 'Aye, I suppose I misled you there, Mr Ward. Didn't want to admit it, like. Fact is, had to move a couple of times, and I never liked getting the cheques, even though I needed them. Pride, it was. But things are changing now. I canna afford pride. I got to think what's best for the bairn. Out there she'd have the best schooling, there'd be wealthy friends, everything she'd be likely to need. In the long run, maybe what's happened is all to the good. It could be for her benefit, like.'

'But what would she be *losing*?' Eric questioned. 'You and Kate are close. Surely she'd be losing the love of a father?'

Cullen looked at Eric directly. There was a dull film of pain in his eyes. He shrugged. 'Aye, but even there . . . Look, Mr Ward, I don't like that bastard Maxwell, and if you ask me my guess would be he had a big hand in the kidnapping of Kate, but the fact is I think Maxwell and Ruth'll maybe get together. Now if that happens, there'd be a man around for Kate then—'

'Not her *father* . . .'

'Maybe in the long run I wouldn't be missed.'

There was a long silence. Cullen was being a realist and it was hurting him badly. Eric felt a vast sympathy for the man. He could appreciate the feeling of helplessness Cullen must be experiencing. It was matched in some degree by Eric's own feelings. Quietly he said, 'What do you want me to do?'

Cullen hesitated. The words needed to be forced out. When they came, his voice was ragged and shaky with emotion. 'I think . . . I think we'd better pack the whole thing in.'

'Pack what in?'

'The search for Kate.'

Eric was silent for a little while. As Cullen took a sip of his whisky Eric watched him: the doggedness and the anger had gone out of the man; his sense of commitment had left him. Eric was puzzled. Something must have happened since last they met, something serious enough to have caused Cullen to review his behaviour, weigh again his emotions against Kate's future well-being. 'Just why have you suddenly changed your mind about taking action against Geraghty and Ruth?' Eric asked.

The telephone buzzed.

Eric ignored the sound. Cullen seemed about to speak but the buzz came again, insistently. A trifle irritated, Eric picked up the phone.

'Yes?'

'Mr Parton is on the line. He says he wants to speak to you, urgently.'

Eric hesitated, glanced at Cullen. 'All right, put him on.'

There was a pause, a click. 'Mr Ward?'

'Jackie, I'm in conference with a client. Is this important?'

'It is, Mr Ward. It's about the killing of Eddie Lister.'

Eric's glance flickered to Cullen. The man was studying his whisky intently, unable to pick up the gist of the conversation. 'All right, go on.'

'There's been a lot of police activity. Seems they've got a witness to the killing.'

'So?'

'I been doing my own checking, Mr Ward. You remember I told you there was another car following Lister? That I had trouble keeping a low profile, that it was almost like a bloody procession across Redheugh? Well, I knew there was something familiar about that car.'

'You recognized it? You said nothing to me at the time.'

'I . . . I wasn't certain. I wanted to make sure.'

Eric recalled the ex-jockey's reticence. He had guessed Parton had been keeping something back from him. 'And now you *are* sure?'

There was a short pause. 'It was a Morris, Mr Ward, a green Morris. It was the one that belongs to Patel Chaddha. I'd spoken to his wife . . . she was the woman who used to pick up Kate Cullen.'

Something cold affected Eric Ward's spine. Perhaps the emotion warned Cullen: his head came up, and he stared at Eric Ward.

'I went to see Mrs Chaddha,' Parton was saying. 'I asked her about the car. She told me the day Lister died she had lent it to a friend.'

'The friend's name?'

'Tony Cullen.'

There was a short silence. Then Eric said, 'Thanks, Jackie, I'll be in touch.' He replaced the phone and looked at the man facing him. Cullen sat frozen, staring at Eric dumbly. Eric hesitated, not knowing what to say, how to start.

The door opened.

He had a vague impression of a disturbed Lizzie, punk hair standing on end, trying to explain. 'I'm sorry, Mr Ward, you were on the phone, and I couldn't reach you and he insisted on . . .'

The girl was being pushed aside. The big frame of Detective-Superintendent Mason was thrusting into the room. His pouched eyes held a glint of malicious pleasure and he was smiling broadly, confidently. 'Well, well, well, the bad birds all together!'

'Mason, I wasn't aware we had an appointment . . .'

'Appointments, forget 'em! Now, your friend Cullen here, *he's* got an appointment. With me. And believe me, it'll take precedence over any chat he wants to have with you.' The malicious smile widened. 'Unless you're going to represent him, of course.'

'Represent him? In what?'

Mason's tone held an edge of triumph. 'Cullen and I need to have a little chat. It could take some time, because he's got some explaining to do. About his involvement in the murder of Eddie Lister. And,' he added, glaring at Eric, 'I think I've already got enough to bring a charge.'

Eric looked at Tony Cullen. The man's face had paled and he sat immobile for several seconds. Then he set down his glass, his hand beginning to shake.

'Well?' Mason said belligerently to Cullen. 'You coming to Morpeth with me and the constable downstairs?'

Cullen looked at Eric; the message in his eyes was plain.

'We're both coming,' Eric Ward said firmly.

2

From the top of the bank Eric could see the Wear looping in a glinting curve past the centre of Sunderland, gleaming away from the Wearmouth Colliery on its right bank and swinging past a shipbuilding yard as it turned south-west to the sea. From this height the moraine of the town's industrial history was exposed: a dependence on shipbuilding and coal-mining—the one industry in decline and the second demanding diminishing manpower resources—had left the predominantly working-class town unable to attract new large-scale employers.

It had also left Jack Cullen high and dry.

Eric watched the old man as he stood at the top of the bank, calling to his racing pigeons. They circled, wary of Eric standing nearby, but as their nervousness faded they swooped in to land at Jack Cullen's feet, flurrying, hopping towards the coop. 'I lose some of the young 'uns,' Cullen said, gesturing towards the mineral railway running below the bank. 'They get frightened off by the whistles of the engines as they pass by.'

Eric had already tried asking him directly about his son, but Cullen's response had been to walk out of the terrace house and climb up the bank to the coop. Now, Eric waited: Jack Cullen was an independent man who would speak when he was ready.

'You spend a lot of time up here?' Eric asked, guessing the old man would talk easily enough about his passion.

'Let the cock birds out, first thing in the morning,' Cullen said and glanced skywards, his seamed old eyes narrowed against the sunlight. He was a short, deep-chested man with an aged skin tanned by sun and wind, and his hands were gnarled and arthritic. He wore a blue suit shiny with wear, and the collar of his shirt, closed by a pearly button, was scuffed and loose-threaded. 'Do a bit of fishing too, though. You can get a codling down there sometimes. In the afternoons I let the hen birds out. And there's the market.' He glanced sideways at Eric, cunningly. 'There's the pension, but I make a bit as well, from selling the birds I breed. Sold a blue cock the other day—hundred and thirty quid.'

He frowned, seeming to regret the confidence suddenly and turned his back on Eric, calling to his birds. Eric began to regret the visit. It was unlikely he would learn anything.

It had been an act almost of desperation, seeking out Tony Cullen's father. The interview at Morpeth had been difficult to handle: Eric had warned Cullen to say little, but Detective-Superintendent Mason had been full of confidence, thrusting and careless in his questioning because, he implied, he already knew the answers. Eric's private interview with Cullen had been less than helpful: the man seemed to be stunned, unable to say very much at all. He seemed careless, unwilling even to consider what his fate might be. And Mason was clear in his own mind: he had a witness who would swear to having seen Cullen at the scene of the crime, and he had been confident enough, later that

evening, to charge Tony Cullen with the murder of Eddie
Lister.

Jackie Parton was already out on the streets, trying to
find out who the witness to the killing might be; he was of
the opinion he could turn up the name in time. For Eric, it
was a different matter: there were no leads he could follow.
There was only the opportunity to try to find out more about
Tony Cullen himself. The neighbours barely knew him; the
family had moved several times, from Cullercoats on the
coast, fifteen miles in to Newcastle, then across the river
to Gateshead. His mother was dead; his father lived in
Sunderland. It was a thin thread.

'I do other things with my time too,' the old man said
abruptly. 'I read. Newspapers, and books. Public library.
History books.' He sat down awkwardly on the bank, fond-
ling the hen bird lovingly in his gnarled hands, cooing at
her in a soft voice, ruffling her feathers in a gentle motion.
'Monkwearmouth, for instance, just a mile away over there
on the north bank. The Venerable Bede lived there most of
his life. And St Michael's Church just there, it was built
nine hundred years ago: one of its vicars was the Duke of
Wellington's brother. Did *you* know that? Hey? You're a
solicitor and I was a miner who took home thirty shillin's a
week, a toolmaker, a shipwright . . . but I know more than
you, I bet.'

'You'll know more about your son than I do,' Eric said,
trying again.

The old man grunted, kissed the hen bird gently. 'More'n
likely, but it won't be much.'

'Did he live here with you in Sunderland?'

'Never. We moved from Cullercoats when his Mam died;
then it were the West End for a while, then Gateshead when
I got a job in the yards at Jarrow. That's when the little
bugger got ideas above his station. I came down here after
he got mixed up with that Irish chit.'

'Ruth Geraghty?'

Jack Cullen did not deign to answer. He rose, took the

bird across to the coop and stood calling at the top of the bank, waiting for the last few birds to swoop home. After a while he said, 'You can trust birds, you knaa. They'll fly far away, but they'll be back. Not like kids. They grow up, think they're their own masters, won't take advice. I washed my hands of my lad when he took up with that girl. I said no good would come of it. Nor did it.'

'I'm just trying to make sense of it all.'

'The kidnapping? Oh aye, I know all about that. I read the papers. It'll have been that old bastard Geraghty, sure as I'm standing here. But there's no point in going on about it. No chance of getting her back. Why bother?'

'Did you ever see her? Kate, I mean?'

'Whaffor?' The old man stared at Eric blankly. 'I told you, the lad went his own way. Stand on his own feet. Nothing to do with me.'

'But she's your granddaughter!'

Jack Cullen seemed baffled by the remark. 'But I told you! Look, it's twelve year and more since I was sent up the road. No more work for me in the yards. I wasn't wanted then, and I'll not be wanted now. I got my house here, and my pension, and my birds and I live on my own. I watch, I know what's going on, but I'm not involved in any of it. I haven't seen the lad in ten years, so you think I'm going to cry now because the kid's been taken to America?'

'And what about the charge that's been made against your son?'

Jack Cullen turned and stared uncomprehendingly at Eric. He scratched a cheek with gnarled fingers; his gaze was clouded as though he was seeking to recall something, the emotions of thirty years, images of a past he had half-forgotten. He had been a man who had once held strong emotions; he had allowed them to atrophy in the reality of old age. 'Murder—aye, now that's some thing . . . When Tony was born, aye, I think mebbe I was proud. Maybe I'd even have killed for him then. But people change, don't they? Grow up . . . Perhaps there was too much of me in

him for us ever to get on.' He grinned in self-awareness.
'I'm an independent, crotchety old bastard. I'm told so,
down at the dole. But I've earned the right, you knaa what
I mean? At my age I've earned the right.'

'So there's nothing you can tell me about Tony that might
help?'

'What's there to tell? Your own kith and kin, they're the
last you know. Why do they say he killed Eddie Lister,
anyway?'

Eric hesitated. 'The motive claimed is that he knew Lister
had taken part in Kate's kidnapping. I've yet to determine
how, but—'

'Well, that wild bastard needed killing, you ask me.'

'Lister? You knew him?'

'Oh aye. Knew *of* him, leastways.' The old man wrinkled
his brow. 'He's a Sunderland man. Lot of talk about him
down at the club. Old folks, you know, when they get
together down at the club, it's all gossip. Prize chrysan-
themums, leeks, fishing, racing pigeons, looking for drift-
wood and seacoal. Talk all the time. And about the
tearaways. Say how it was different when we were kids. But
it wasn't. No, it wasn't any different.'

'So what's been the gossip about Lister?' Eric asked.

'Well, I'll tell yer. He always was a yobbo, but recently
he tried to show respectable, moved out of Sunderland, up
to Newcastle, but he hadn't changed, and he still worked
back here in the town. Story is he was in with Ted Mansell,
knocking over that garage six months back, but there was
nothing the polis could lay on him.'

'You say he worked here in Sunderland?'

The old man stared at him thoughtfully. 'That's right.
Worked for Chad Cowell, he did, on and off.'

'Doing what?'

'You name it; I can't. Windmill Leisure Centre. Run by
Chad Cowell. That's a laugh! Council need their heads
seeing to . . .'

*

The music was loud and strident in the half-darkened room; the spotlight on the stage was erratic and badly positioned so that occasional howls of protest rose from the more vociferous of the audience when the girl inadvertently stepped out of the circle of light. Her gyrations were obvious and owed little to art but now that she had stripped to a G-string the audience cared little for that. She was in her late thirties and had dyed blonde hair; her waistline was beginning to thicken but the lunch-time drinkers were well aware that the afternoon club strippers were far from professional: most of them were married women whose husbands were unemployed and who were seeking another source of income. The husbands didn't seem to mind after the first few occasions, Jackie Parton had heard, and the women themselves seemed to enjoy the independence it gave them in their male-dominated society.

The man seated beside Jackie finished his pint of Newcastle Brown as the act ended, the blonde woman sliding off crabwise with a scattering of clothes draped modestly against her body. There were a few catcalls, and Jackie's companion grinned. 'The boys never get too rough. I tell you, Jackie, you want to go to one of the hen nights, when the male strippers are in. Why, man, they all but tear him to pieces! No inhibitions, none at all, and cackling like crazy! Decent women, I tell you, but all together with a male stripper . . .'

'Has he come in yet?'

For a moment the man's gaze was glazed with incomprehension. 'Oh, sorry, man. I hadna been watchin'—concentratin' on the show, like. Hold on . . .' He looked about him, scanning the bar at the back of the room. He nodded. 'Aye, he's in. Look, over there, the feller with the blue and white shirt.'

'Thanks. I owe you,' Jackie said.

'Anything for a mate. But watch yourself, hey?'

'I'll do that.'

He rose and walked towards the bar. The music had

started again, a Beatles number, and the next girl had come out on the stage to do vaguely obscene things with an uninterested snake. A few suggestions called to her proposed even more impossible gyrations: she took them with a fixed smile and a firm grip on the dazed serpent.

The man in the blue and white shirt was leaning against the bar facing the stage, little eyes shining, red face sweating. He barely glanced at Jackie as he approached; his attention was riveted upon the girl. Jackie ordered two pints of beer and then turned to the man at the bar.

'One of these is for you,' Jackie said.

'Hey?'

'You're Ferdy Newton, aren't you? One of these is for you.'

The bulky, middle-aged man turned around slowly to stare Jackie up and down. 'What the hell should you be buying a beer for and giving it to me? I don't know you.'

'Jackie Parton.'

The piggy little eyes widened in momentary surprise, and then took on a malicious gleam of satisfaction. 'Oh aye, Jackie Parton, is it? Well I'll certainly take a drink off you, you little bugger. Come to tell me you been warned off, is that it? Making amends, as they say.'

'Warned off? How do you mean?'

Ferdy Newton took a long drink and wiped his mouth with the back of his hand. 'Aw, come on, friend! I know you been making inquiries about me, sniffin' around some of the punters, trying to nail me with something, working for Sam Turriff. You finally got the message, did you? I warned that solicitor chap, Ward, when he was poking his nose around Phil Heckles, told him if he didn't get off my back, there'd be trouble. He's taken the hint, hey? Pulled you off, and you're trying to square things. Well, I don't bear grudges and—'

'You got it wrong, Ferdy,' Parton said, placing his elbows on the bar. 'I just bought you the drink because I hear you've become a public-spirited man.'

The music thundered to a crescendo and Ferdy Newton's glance was dragged towards the stage by the roar of applause at the snake's attempts to avoid unnatural entanglements. His glance slid back, unwillingly. 'Public-spirited? What the hell you talking about?'

Jackie Parton smiled. 'Well, I'll tell you. I hear a local roughneck by the name of Eddie Lister was knifed the other day. They charged a feller called Tony Cullen with the murder. Confident, the coppers are. Because they got someone who could identify the killer, someone who says it was Tony Cullen. So I been asking around, trying to find out who blew the whistle on Cullen and put the coppers on his back. Surprise, surprise, a little bird hops up and tells me it was one of Sam Turriff's ticket-men. Name of Ferdy Newton. So I thought I'd buy him a drink.'

Something had happened to Ferdy Newton's face. His sandy, thinning hair seemed to bristle as he stared at Parton, but uncertainty moved deep in his eyes and his questing nose was raised, as though sniffing for danger. He frowned, calculating situations, weighing them, probing his own mind for reasons, and then just as suddenly as his tension had risen, so it was gone and he relaxed. He reached for the pint Jackie had bought and took a stiff drink, then laughed, shaking his head. 'O' course. I got it now. You been workin' for that solicitor Ward, sussing out Sam Turriff's operation, but Ward's got a new client now, is that it? Cullen's taken him on to defend him on a murder charge! Well, lemme give you a piece of good advice that you can pass on to that bastard Ward. He doesn't stand a chance. Cullen did Eddie Lister in and that's all there is to it. He had the motive— the coppers told me that Cullen blamed Lister for snatching his kid—he was there at the time of the murder, and I seen him leaving. Ward hasna got a chance, I'm telling you!'

'What were *you* doing in the area, Ferdy?'

Newton laughed again. 'Don't think you can try to put one of those on me, Parton. I was around there on my legitimate business.' He laughed again, but it lacked some

of the confidence of a few moments ago. 'I was on Sam
Turriff's business down among the flats. I'd parked my car
in the main street because it's easier to cross the wasteland
to some of the pads, to get to my clients. And that's how I
came to see it.'

'See what?'

'Cullen, running out of the block like a pack of cats was
after him. I didn't pay too much attention to it at the time.
I mean, people runnin' around there, that's nothing new. I
always keep a sharp eye open myself, though there's not
many stupid enough to try to mug one of Sam's ticket-men.
I mean, it'd be the river, wouldn't it?'

'Did you know Cullen, then?' Parton asked.

Newton shook his head. 'Naw, didn't know him. Just saw
him runnin' and wouldn't have paid no mind to it, like I
say, except that the crazy bastard, when I was walking
down to my own car he comes driving around the corner
like a maniac. He nearly had me down; I had to leap for
the wall, and I was mad as hell, shouting at him. He didn't
give a damn. But I saw the car and I got his number.'

'That was quick thinking, Ferdy.'

Newton scowled. 'That's the way it happened.'

'The car came from behind you, scared the pants off you,
but you had the presence of mind to recognize the driver as
the man you'd seen running shortly before, you noted the
make of the car *and* its number plate?' Jackie shook his
head. 'Sounds like you're romanticizing, lad.'

'That's the way it happened,' Newton said slowly, his
narrow eyes fixed thoughtfully on Jackie Parton's face. 'You
trying to make something out?'

'The police believe you?'

'They charged Cullen.'

'It'll never stick in court.'

'That's their problem, not mine. I got nothing to do with
all that.' He hesitated, peering at the ex-jockey. 'Fact is,
I'm what the fuzz calls a disinterested witness. I didn't know
this character Cullen; I never had anything to do with him;

he was there, I fingered him, and that's all there is to it.'

Jackie Parton sipped his beer. 'Tell me,' he said softly, 'how did the police happen to find you, with this story?'

Ferdy Newton turned half away. He seemed a little unsure of himself again, hesitating as he considered the words he was about to utter, weighing them for danger. 'I phoned in.'

'You phoned the police? You mean you knew Eddie Lister was dead? You'd seen the body?'

A line of perspiration had gathered on Newton's upper lip. 'Naw. You got it wrong. I phoned in to make a complaint about that crazy bastard's driving. I tell you, he nearly killed me! I wasn't standing for that. So I phoned the local nick, hour or so later, and then next day they all bloody descended on me like an avalanche. I didn't know what the hell it was all about, not then. Once I told them I could identify the car they was over the moon. But I hadn't seen no body, and I didn't know he'd snuffed anybody. I was just reporting a mad dog driver.' He turned his face to Jackie Parton. 'And you can make what the hell you like of that, but that's the way it was.'

Next moment he had shouldered his way past Jackie and was stalking out of the club as the midday drinkers gave one final roar of applause for the girl and the surprised yellow and green snake.

3

The sign proclaimed the availability of classes in art, photography and embroidery, music appreciation, languages and discussion groups. Yoga, music and movement and swimming tuition was also available, with special classes for the over-sixties. The building itself was stark concrete, blocks surmounted by glass slotted windows; at the far end the windows were longer and tinted blue, and there was the noise of swimmers, but here at the entrance the grey forbidding appearance of the leisure centre was lightened by bright carpets and green fern.

Eric had left Jackie in the car outside, parked where he had a view of the entrance. There was a receptionist on duty, explaining to an elderly couple that the entrance fee of 25p also gave you tea and biscuits and the craze of the moment was for *thés dansants*. 'It's great fun,' she was explaining, 'elegant, lots of turns, and hand-clapping. You'll enjoy it.'

She didn't add that it might help them forget the grim Victorian terraces that formed the approach to the oddly sited leisure centre, Eric thought.

When she had persuaded the couple to enrol, the young receptionist turned to Eric. 'Can I help you?'

'I'd like to see Mr Cowell.'

She wasn't sure she liked that. She pondered the matter for a moment, teasing her lower lip with her teeth and then she smiled uncertainly. 'I'll see if he's in.'

'My name is Ward,' Eric supplied. 'I'm a solicitor—and I want to talk to him about Eddie Lister.'

Something flared in her widening eyes for a moment, then she turned away to the phone. There was a brief conversation. She replaced the receiver, managed a nervous smile and rose, adjusting her skirt self-consciously. 'Perhaps you'd like to follow me, Mr Ward.'

She led the way across the foyer towards the staircase at the far end. On the second floor the corridor was carpeted discreetly in pale fawn colours: from the window there was an uninspiring view of wasteland and car parks. She tapped on the door at the end of the corridor, announced his name, and withdrew.

Chad Cowell was standing in front of his desk, thighs supporting his weight as he leaned carelessly back against the desk edge. He was about thirty-five years old, deep-chested, the short-sleeved shirt emphasizing the muscular development of his upper arms. His legs were chunky and powerful, his hair cut short. He gave the impression of an athlete who was now careful that he did not run to seed, but there was a fleshiness about his jaw which suggested he was perhaps not being careful enough. His smile was friendly as he greeted Ward, but it was a fixed smile that had not arrived naturally. Perhaps he had had to face too many local authority committees to get this job. A physical background, and now a desk job in some comfort. Not very well paid, but welcome. There was no welcome in his eyes: they were slate-grey and cool, appraising, but with a sharp suspicion lurking in their depths.

'What can I do for you, Mr Ward? Not often we get lawyers around the leisure centre.'

'You must get some who come in to get fit, surely?' Eric asked.

'But I gather you're not here to talk about what we have to offer.'

There was a short silence as Eric stared at the man. Chad Cowell was nervous and knew he had made an immediate mistake. 'You *know* why I'm here?' Eric asked quietly.

'Of course not,' Cowell struggled. 'I merely meant . . . well, you're clearly not dressed to be *active* at the centre, and . . .' He decided to make no further attempt to cover his confusion. He turned, walked behind his desk for the psychological protection it gave him. 'I don't have a great deal of time, I'm afraid, Mr Ward. I have other appointments . . .'

Eric nodded. 'I won't waste your time, then.' He glanced around the room, noting the filing cabinets, the desk-top computer. 'You're clearly a busy man. I just wanted to ask you a few questions.'

'About?'

'Eddie Lister.'

Chad Cowell had been expecting it. He leaned back in his chair, confidently, and shrugged, spread his hands wide. 'What about Lister?'

'You know he's been murdered.'

'Of course. I read the papers.'

'And he *was* employed by you.'

'There's about sixty people employed here.'

'What do I gather from that?' Eric asked.

'Just that I don't know very much about half of them—cleaners, office staff, caretakers, swimming instructors—'

'And in that half you include Eddie Lister?'

'That's right,' Cowell said with a gleam of malicious satisfaction in his eyes. 'I don't think there's anything I can usefully tell you about Lister.'

'You knew he had something of a . . . wild background?'

'People who get murdered often do.'

'There's a rumour he was involved recently in an attempt to rob a garage.'

'Rumours run around; garages get robbed; this is a *leisure* centre, Mr Ward.'

'That employs some odd people.'

Chad Cowell pursed his lips thoughtfully and stared at Eric. He shook his head. 'Your next question is going to be why I employed Eddie Lister. All right, let me spell it out to you. Sunderland is no country town. It's a raw city with a hell of a lot of frustration and a hell of a lot of unemployment. Some of the frustration gets worked off on a Saturday night: one of the reasons I got this job three years ago was because I convinced people that I could get a lot of the frustration among young people worked off in this place.'

'That's a reason to employ a man like Lister?'

Cowell bridled. 'You're out of touch, Ward! I told you this is no pussyfooting area! We want to pull the *community* in here—from *thés dansants* to water polo. But inevitably, with that kind of policy, you're going to get an element that'll cause trouble. We're committed here to serving a dying community, to giving that community a new lease of life, some excitement, some pleasure, some healthy activity. We don't want that spoiled by yobboes. So we need a few people who can cope with trouble, as and when it arises.'

'From middle-aged couples?'

'From teenagers who want to take the place apart, dammit!'

The anger that suddenly spilled through had removed some of the carefully rehearsed sincerity from Cowell's tone. He had convinced a committee somewhere he had the commitment to social care that was needed in this job; he had not convinced Eric Ward. Slowly, Eric said, 'So you employed Lister as a bouncer?'

Cowell hesitated. 'I suppose . . . well, something like that.'

'And Mansell?'

The hesitation was fractionally longer. 'What about Mansell?'

'Isn't he also employed by you? In a similar capacity?'

'I don't see—'

'It was Mansell who Lister is supposed to have been involved with in that attempted garage robbery.'

'What the hell is this? Lister, Mansell, garage robbery— all this has nothing to do with me, rumour, suggestions—'

'That's the point,' Eric insisted. 'Rumour, whispers. There's more than one would expect about a place concerned with community service, Mr Cowell. You employ two people who have criminal records; they have vaguely defined jobs; one of them has recently been murdered—and I'm pretty certain that same person was involved in the kidnapping of a young girl in Newcastle. The thing is, there were two people in the car when she was snatched. I just wonder who the other man was?'

Chad Cowell stared at Eric, silent for several seconds. His eyes were flinty and he clenched his fists, the muscles in his upper arm tensing. 'I think you're unwise, Mr Ward, trying to tie me in with anything Eddie Lister might have been up to.'

'I'm not,' Eric said innocently. 'I'm simply trying to discover what you know about Lister. And his activities. You say you know nothing. I find that hard to credit.'

'Mr Ward—'

'You half expected me today, didn't you? You knew why I'd be coming. I wonder who warned you?'

'I don't know what the hell you're talking about!'

Eric nodded slowly, eyeing Chad Cowell. The tension was still apparent in the man's upper body, but there was a wariness there too, a cautious waiting. 'Oh yes,' Eric said softly, 'I think you were warned I might be paying a call that would be less than social. Because you know a lot of people around the Tyne and Wear, don't you? The wrong sort of people, some might say.'

'I run a leisure centre, nothing more.'

'That's not what people say. Rumour—*persistent* rumour —suggests that there's more to this club than meets the eye. The odd thing is the police don't seem to have done much about it. Perhaps the rumours haven't reached their ears. Or perhaps there's one or two who've had their ears stuffed with paper money. Old age pensioners, now, they don't get their ears stuffed. And they hear things. Gossip. Old people love it, indulge in it. And they use this centre, see people come here, young kids, shaky, nervous, in a state. But sometimes those kids go away again more settled, high even.'

'What the hell are you trying to say?'

'Say? I'm just repeating what I've heard. That there's more to this leisure centre than the council would believe. That there's a certain amount of drug-peddling goes on here. That it's a known centre where youngsters can make a score. That maybe you know all about it—even encourage it. After all, you do employ roughnecks like Lister—'

'I don't have to listen to this!'

'No, but you haven't thrown me out yet.'

'All this talk about drugs, it's crazy, gossip. I can't be held responsible for what kids get up to.'

'*Knowing* is enough, Mr Cowell. Responsibility, ah well, if it can be shown . . .' Eric stared at Cowell, smiling coldly, 'Odd, isn't it, that you *haven't* thrown me out yet? But maybe it's because you knew I didn't come here to talk about drugs. Perhaps you want to know how close I am to identifying those involved with Kate Cullen's kidnapping. Because maybe you were involved; maybe you'll even know something more than you care to admit about the murder of Eddie Lister.'

'Now look here!' Chad Cowell's mask had slipped now as he rose menacingly to his feet. He was shorter than Eric but he was a powerful man and his belligerence was thrusting through the control he had exercised so far. 'This is my club. I don't give a damn about rumours. You come up with something you can prove, then prove it. But there's no way you can, and there's *no* way you can tie me in with Lister's death. I got nothing to do with that, and there's no way I'm going to stay here listening to you any more. I can't help you with this business. I just employed Lister and that was that. This interview is over.'

Eric smiled slightly and turned away. He glanced around the room as though admiring it. He nodded towards the desk-top computer. 'Modern.'

'Useful,' Cowell growled. 'We can timetable on it, and keep our accounts straight.'

'The software you use . . . I imagine it will be customized.'

'We use special programs.'

'Tell me, when you get a machine in like this and develop software, the first thing you do is to get a firm in to do an analysis for you, isn't it? I mean, to determine your systems, advise you, develop the software for you.'

'That's right,' Cowell said warily. 'Now, if you don't mind—'

'Takes some time to sort that out, I imagine. A fair number of consultations, I would expect. Who . . . ah . . . who did you get to do your systems analysis, and develop the software?'

Cowell was silent.

Eric walked across to the machine. There was a package containing a floppy disk lying on the desk top. He picked it up, read the inscription and logo, and smiled. 'Ah, a Newcastle firm, I see.'

'Goodbye, Mr Ward,' Cowell said harshly.

The girl at reception was busy advising an elderly couple on the excitements of *thés dansants* again as Eric left.

He walked out into the street. Jackie Parton was sitting in the car, waiting. Eric slid in beside him. He felt vaguely depressed. The interview had not been very productive, partly because of his own distrust of Cowell and the feeling that the man had known he was likely to call. It added to puzzles already buzzing in his mind. There were links he could not perceive.

'You get anything?' Parton asked.

'Not a lot. He simply claims he employed Lister as a bouncer. Didn't know anything about him. But . . .'

'Yes?'

Eric shook his head. 'I'm not sure. It's a bit tenuous, but . . . Cowell's got a desk-top computer. The software is produced by a Newcastle firm, Maxwell Computer Services, Ltd.'

'So?'

'The company is owned by Ruth Geraghty's boyfriend, Peter Maxwell.'

Jackie Parton screwed up his eyes, peering at the street. He was silent for a little while. 'That's a bit of a long shot, Mr Ward.'

'It could be just coincidence. But Maxwell *is* Ruth's boyfriend; there has clearly been contact between Maxwell and Chad Cowell; and Cowell employed Lister, who's been identified as the man who snatched Kate Cullen. As I say, it *could* be coincidence . . .'

Jackie Parton sighed. 'I know what you mean. Fact is, I can add to the *coincidences*.'

'How do you mean?'

'A little while ago, while you were still inside with Chad Cowell, I saw someone I know leaving the leisure centre. It explained to me how Lister was fingered.'

'I don't understand,' Eric said.

'Lister was identified as being in the kidnap car. Now I get the connection. A little while ago I saw a young friend of mine leaving the club. She was in a hurry, but she looked happy. Drug-happy. On a recent high.'

Eric thought for a few moments, then stared at Jackie Parton. 'The girl . . . Davinia?'

'The very same, Mr Ward, the very same.'

CHAPTER 5

1

It was outside Durham Gaol, in 1865, that Matthew Atkinson had been 'turned off'. It had caused quite a sensation. When the executioner slipped the bolt Atkinson fell—but the rope snapped. Atkinson fell heavily, and 'some concern was expressed that he might have hurt himself'. He rose after a little while, 'to a ragged cheer' from the crowd, unscathed apart from a red mark on his neck. They had to wait twenty minutes while a new rope was obtained. The nervous hangman had decided to use a short drop this time; his inexperience led to Atkinson strangling to death, slowly kicking his heels. Twenty thousand people watched the performance.

Times had changed. No public hangings now, and no large crowds outside the gaol—just cars parked in the heat of the summer afternoon and a shimmering haze above the solid tower of the cathedral. The arrest of Tony Cullen for the murder of Eddie Lister had caused no sensation large enough to draw crowds.

Eric Ward had protested against the holding of Cullen at Durham: it was an over-reaction on the part of Superintendent Mason in his view. Morpeth Gaol would have been sound enough, but Mason had seemed to want to extract maximum satisfaction from the arrest—and publicity. Durham Gaol was well enough known for its notorious D Wing for violent prisoners: perhaps there would be some guilt by association for Tony Cullen.

Eric drove the twenty miles from Newcastle in the early afternoon, taking the road through Pity Me and Framwellgate Moor to avoid the city centre and was at the gaol in good time for the appointment with Cullen. His client greeted him in subdued fashion. Prison experience had obviously sobered him and deepened the depression he had seemed to be suffering from when Eric had left him at Morpeth. But it was time for Eric to get some answers.

'All right, Tony, first of all, the obvious question, and one I've not put to you before. Did you stick that knife in Eddie Lister?'

Cullen's eyes were shadowed and his mouth unhappy, but he shook his head slowly and determinedly. 'Mr Ward, I swear to you that I didn't kill him.'

'But you were there?'

'I . . . I went there. I followed him. But when I found him he was already kicking his life out. He was all but dead. Mr Ward, I swear—'

'Let's start at the beginning, Tony.' Eric took a deep breath. 'Did you know that Eddie Lister had been involved in the kidnapping of your daughter?'

'I didn't *know*, Mr Ward . . .' Cullen shook his head again, as though trying to clear it and clarify the emotions that had affected him then, and now. 'I got a phone call—'

'From whom?'

Cullen shrugged. 'An old man . . . I knew him from way back but there's been no contact for some years. He knew my old man. He was called Goalie Edwards.'

'Go on.'

'He was drunk. Maudlin. He was all but cryin' down the phone. He was babbling about families and how if he'd been a father he'd have killed anyone who tried to snatch his kid. I didn't understand at first, was goin' to cut it short, like, and then he told me he'd been talkin' to Jackie Parton. I began to listen then.'

'So this was after Parton met Edwards at the pub?'

'Aye. About half past three in the afternoon. It soon got through to me. Goalie Edwards had sussed out that Jackie Parton was asking after this character Lister because of Kate's kidnapping. Edwards had told Jackie where Lister lived. He gave me the same information over the phone.'

'And?'

Tony Cullen looked up. His eyes were hollow, anxiety-ridden, as he thought back over the reasons for his own behaviour. 'Mr Ward, what was I to do? I was desperate about Kate. I heard Goalie Edwards out and he was talking wild, drink-fuddled, but some of what he said made sense. If you'd had a kid, what would you have done? The police wouldn't help, I felt on my own, and Goalie's drunken suggestions—'

'You should have contacted me, Tony.'

'Aye. Well.'

'So what *did* you do?'

Cullen shrugged aimlessly. 'I was in a stupor for a while. And then I got angry, yeah, even murderous at the time. I went out, called on Mrs Chaddha, asked her if I could borrow the car. She agreed. I drove out to the address Goalie Edwards had given me. Then I sat there, frozen, not knowing what to do. I was still there, uncertain, when I saw this man come from Lister's place. Damn it, I didn't even *know* it was Lister, I'd never seen him, but when he got in the VW I followed him.'

'And so did Jackie Parton,' Eric said grimly.

'I didn't know that at the time.'

'You caused him problems.'

'Yeh . . . I wasn't thinking straight, Mr Ward, and I was getting more and more angry. Anyway, when Lister pulled up near the flats I went into the side-street and parked and then got out looking for him. Most of these blocks are deserted. It was the noise that finally brought me to him.'

'Noise?'

'There was a shouting, a stamping, then running feet, somebody arguing, high voices. I went up the stairs careful. Then I heard the groaning.'

'Lister?'

'He was in the corner. On his side. The blood looked black, like, you know. His eyes was closed, face twisted. He was hurting.'

'Did you go near him?'

'Had to, didn't I? Got some blood on my shoe as well. But he was *hurtin'*, Mr Ward.'

And there would be forensic evidence to link Cullen with the scene apart from Ferdy Newton's testimony, Eric thought grimly. 'So what happened then?'

Tony Cullen looked around at the grey walls of the narrow room. He grimaced, as though he were seeing them for the first time. There was a line of perspiration along his upper lip. 'I . . . I got scared, didn't I? Panicked, more like. Maybe I could have done something for him—'

'Nothing. That was a mortal wound, Tony.'

'I was panicked, even so. I just run out of there, like a kid. Down the steps, charging across the waste land, dived into the car, shakin', like. I couldn't move then, maybe five, ten minutes I was shakin' so bad. Then I could see him again and I was scared and I got the hell out of there.'

Eric waited for a few moments, and then said gently, 'You drove away and returned the car to Mrs Chaddha but said nothing to her or anyone else.'

'I was scared, Mr Ward.'

'You said nothing to me.'

'In your office?' Cullen shook his head in desperation. 'It all seemed so . . . hopeless. I mean, the man who helped steal Kate, he was dead and I didn't understand, and Geraghty's got all the money in the world and all the power —I just wanted to give up, Mr Ward, I was finished, and I just didn't want to know any more.'

'And what about Ferdy Newton?'

'What do you mean?'

'You almost ran him down.'

'I don't remember.'

'He says you almost killed him when you drove off after Lister died.'

'Mr Ward, I don't recall, but you got to remember I was scared, panicked, I don't even remember driving across the river or anything. It could have happened, maybe it did, but I don't remember.'

'Maybe it did,' Eric said quietly, 'and maybe it didn't . . . Do you know Chad Cowell, Tony?'

Cullen shook his head dumbly.

'I've been to see your father.' When Cullen raised his head in surprise, Eric went on, 'I thought there might be some way he could help, even if you and he haven't been in touch for some years.'

'He didn't rate my marrying Ruth. The old man was probably right, way things turned out.'

'He did give me some useful information, and hints, nevertheless. First, he told me Lister worked for Chad Cowell in Sunderland. Second, that the leisure centre run by Cowell has been the subject of some gossip.'

'I don't understand,' Cullen said in a bewildered tone.

'Lister was a hard man. Cowell, it seems from inquiries I've made in the last few days, could be using the leisure centre as a front for illegal activities. Just *how* illegal I've yet to determine. But it could involve drug pushing. More important, he's had some dealings with Peter Maxwell.'

'*Maxwell?*' Cullen's tone had sharpened as his head came up, his glazed eyes revealing a new interest. 'Where does he fit into this?'

'I'm not yet sure.' Eric hesitated. 'Have you anything more to tell me, anything that might lead to discovering who *did* kill Lister?'

Cullen shook his head. 'I didn't see anyone. Don't even recall seeing Ferdy Newton.'

'Well, I think maybe it's all linked in some way to Kate's kidnapping.'

'I don't understand, Mr Ward.'

Eric shrugged. 'It's only a vague hypothesis, Tony. But if we accept what we have as *links* rather than mere coincidences, it could go something like this. Ruth wanted Kate with her. She contacted her father. He talked things over with Peter Maxwell. They entered a conspiracy. One of the jobs Maxwell was doing was a systems analysis for Chad Cowell. The manager of the leisure centre is involved with certain other activities, and uses men with a criminal background. A few hints, a private conversation or two and Maxwell is introduced to Eddie Lister. Maxwell pays Lister to snatch Kate. The job is done and Kate is spirited away to Ireland. And then a problem arises.'

'Problem?'

'I start putting pressure on, in your behalf, and at the same time Lister gets greedy.'

'He wants more money?'

'I think so. He puts the bite on Peter Maxwell maybe, or even directly upon Geraghty.'

'Geraghty wouldn't like that.'

'I believe it,' Eric said soberly. 'Anyway, either way, once the contact is made Geraghty—or maybe Maxwell—suggests a meeting, in a quiet place. Lister goes, confidently. And ends up with a knife in his stomach. The thing is . . . do you believe Maxwell would be capable of such a thing?'

Cullen hesitated, doubt twitching at his mouth. 'I wish I could say so. But no. Geraghty, now . . .'

'Yes?'

'He wouldn't do it himself. But he might be mad enough to pay for it to be done.'

'And Ferdy Newton?'

Cullen grunted. 'He's a *ticket-man*, Mr Ward. He can act tough and sound tough, but he's mainly mouth. He relies on Sam Turriff's musclemen behind him if punters don't pay up. He doesn't take the gloves off himself.'

'So what's his connection with all this?' Eric asked. 'Why would he display this rush of public spirit, even put himself in some jeopardy by admitting he was in the vicinity—if he was at all—and point the finger at you?'

'I don't know, Mr Ward,' Cullen said, shaking his head, 'I really don't know . . . unless . . .'

Eric waited. There was a germ of a reason in his own mind but he wanted to see whether the same thought would occur to Tony Cullen. He waited and saw Cullen's eyes widen as he thought the thing through.

'There is one possibility, Mr Ward, now I think of it. Ferdy Newton probably *was* in the vicinity. Maybe he even saw me. But he's a *ticket-man*. Normally he wouldn't get involved—but for one thing. Money.' He glared angrily up at Eric. 'You see, the ticket-men are scroungers. They scrape a living off other people, like ticks on a sheep's back. And they're in heavy with the likes of Sam Turriff. They have to come up with the goods; they have to produce the money he expects or they're likely to end up in the same place as the punter who doesn't raise the cash he owes. So they are vicious, hard in pushing for the money. And if they don't produce, they're in trouble too.'

'Go on.'

'And the other thing is, travelling around, talking to people, listening, meeting all sorts, they get to *hear* things. They get to know what's happening, what's going on.'

'Like who might have been behind the kidnapping of Kate Cullen,' Eric suggested softly.

There was a new urgency in Cullen's demeanour. He bobbed his head excitedly. 'That's it, Mr Ward. It makes sense. Maybe Ferdy had picked up a few rumours, heard of Peter Maxwell's connection with Kate's kidnapping. Maybe he *did* see me run off the estate; perhaps he put two and two together later when he heard Lister had been killed, and got worried. I'm into Sam Turriff for almost a thousand quid . . . Ferdy would want to put that right. One way to do it would be to go to Maxwell, agree to slam the thing squarely on me, get me out of Geraghty's and Maxwell's hair—and pay off Sam Turriff with even a bit to spare. It makes sense, Mr Ward!'

'It's based on a number of suppositions,' Eric warned.

'But it could be the truth, even so. You'll look into it?'

'I'll look into it.' Eric rose to leave. 'I have to say, however, that there's still one basic problem. Ferdy Newton claims he phoned in to complain about your driving. But there had to be *another* call—an anonymous one—telling the police that someone had been murdered in the tower block. The question is, who made that call?'

Cullen furrowed his brow. He had no answer. Neither did Eric. He gathered up his papers and walked to the door. 'I'll be in touch as soon as I can,' he promised.

'Mr Ward?'

'Yes?'

Tony Cullen grimaced. He seemed to be struggling with himself, finding great difficulty in getting out the words, but yet desperate in his loneliness to force them out. 'Mr Ward . . . do you think . . . do you think my Da would come to see us?'

Eric had a vision of a deep-chested, gnarled old man on the hillside above Sunderland, watching his pigeons wheeling back to their coop, white-fluttering against the darkening evening sky. A self-centred, dogged old man, who had thrust the past, and emotion, behind him and who now only lived for the pigeons that filled his waking hours. He stood and looked at Tony Cullen sympathetically. 'I wouldn't count on it, Tony,' he said.

'Naw,' Cullen said with a note of resignation and despondency in his voice. 'You're right. I shouldna count on it, should I?'

2

The week passed quickly.

Eric had a long conversation with the Morcomb Estates lawyer Mark Fenham: the negotiations with Liam Geraghty for the Northumberland estates had now been formally ended and Fenham was peeved that so much work had been for nothing. He seemed to take it personally and vented his spleen over the phone to Eric. He was young; he would learn. Eric made no attempt to explain the background to the negotiations to him, nor the reasons for their breakdown.

The latter part of the week he spent in lengthy discussions with a marine insurance company which was negotiating a retainer with him. He was subjected to discourses that informed him that marine insurance went back to at least 215 BC since there was a reference to it in Livy. He suffered it for one very good reason: a substantial retainer and the opportunity to strengthen the commercial side of his business.

Jackie Parton had been given a job to do, but had not been in touch with Eric all week. On Friday morning, Eric had completed the papers on the Sam Turriff case and made his way out to Longbenton to talk matters over with Nick Hawthorne before service of the papers.

Hawthorne leaned back in his chair and puffed at his pipe with every sign of evident satisfaction. He scratched his shaggy hair and smiled. 'So you think we've got enough on the bastard?'

'I reckon so,' Eric replied. 'You've had time now to read the statement made by Tony Cullen. It give us enough detail to nail Turriff through his agents, and enough to persuade the OFT to remove his licence.'

'The Office of Fair Trading has never been noted for its speed of action,' Hawthorne grunted.

'They'll act on this. You'll send a copy to Mr Fraser?'

'I will. If only to send a bolt up his backside. Right, so we got enough to make the OFT act, but what about our own prosecution?'

'Cullen will appear in court and testify to back up the deposition. There's enough evidence here to have Turriff convicted of at least two criminal offences. He'll not get a prison term, of course—'

'The bastard!'

'—but there'll be a hefty fine, loss of licence, and my guess is one less loan shark on the Tyneside waterfront.'

'And that,' Hawthorne said smugly, 'gives me a great deal of satisfaction.' He hesitated, frowned, then glanced uncertainly at Eric. 'There's just one thing.'

'Yes?'

'Cullen.'

Eric waited. He could guess what was coming. He watched Hawthorne as the big man's coarse features struggled to overcome the anxiety he felt. 'He's on a murder charge,' he said at last.

'That's right.'

'It won't make a difference? To his appearing in court against Turriff, I mean?'

Eric hesitated. 'It'll make a difference, yes. It may make appearance impossible. But that presupposes Cullen is convicted of the murder. We're a long way from that yet.'

'But either way, he'll be in custody when the Turriff prosecution comes on.'

'That's likely. And it will pose difficulties.'

'But you think we should still proceed immediately?'

'That's my opinion.'

Hawthorne sighed, and nodded. 'Well, I guess we'll go ahead. I've been waiting for a long time to get Turriff . . . You're acting for Cullen, of course. How are things going?'

'There's a circumstantial case against him, but it's not watertight.'

'*Did* he kill this character Lister?'

'I'm pretty sure he didn't.'

'He had motive, I hear.' Lamely Hawthorne added, 'We get a lot of gossip in the field.'

'If you mean Lister's being involved in Kate's kidnapping, yes, he had motive.'

'And it was Ferdy Newton who put the finger on Cullen,' Nick Hawthorne said thoughtfully. 'Humph! Just shows what a small place the world is.'

'Tyneside's small enough, certainly,' Eric agreed.

'But I mean, Ferdy Newton, one of Sam Turriff's ticket-men, being the witness against Tony Cullen, one of the punters on his own books! Out of character, that, Ferdy squealing on someone who owes Sam Turriff money.'

'We think,' Eric said slowly, 'his perjury—if he *is* lying —will not leave him out of pocket.'

Hawthorne's brown eyes widened at the thought. He sucked on his pipe for a moment and then said, 'You think he's been got at . . . or covered himself, got paid off maybe even to shop young Cullen. It's a thought . . . Even so, I have to say I still think it's a bit out of character. Newton's not the kind who'd help the law under any circumstances. I think I told you before, he comes from a family of tear-aways, but Ferdy had two characteristics. The one was always obvious: he kept as far away from the police as he could while still indulging in whatever petty crime he could turn his hand to. And the other characteristic was an unusual one: he looked after his grandma and the rest of the bloody family, too. I could see him shopping Cullen for family reasons, but for money is another story. I mean, he's put himself in the legal limelight with a vengeance: it must have been a hell of a lot of money that would make him turn against his faith like that!'

'It's a theory, anyway.'

'Mmm. And you're keeping an eye on him, I imagine.'

Just that. Or, to be more precise, Jackie Parton was keeping an eye on Ferdy Newton. But Jackie had not phoned in all week.

*

It was a wearying business.

Jackie Parton knew the West End like the back of his hand and the rest of Newcastle and its environs almost as well. It enabled him to maintain a low profile in the trailing of Ferdy Newton. It meant he was able to take short cuts, travel parallel streets, make his way through cuts and alleys in the sure knowledge that he would not lose the track of his quarry. It was imperative that Ferdy Newton did not realize he was being trailed and Jackie Parton took every reasonable precaution. But perhaps he had been *too* reasonable for there were two occasions when he lost the ticket-man.

It bothered him. He had the feeling all along that Newton was taking particular care not to be followed: the pattern of his behaviour demonstrated it. Jackie was sufficiently skilled and knowledgeable about the neighbourhood to be able to counteract this, but on two occasions Newton had defeated him. Deliberately.

The excess of caution on the ticket-man's part puzzled Parton. Ferdy Newton spent most of his time doing his rounds, calling on punters, touting for custom for Sam Turriff, slipping into the occasional betting shop for a bet on the 'ponies', stopping by at lunch-time for a few beers in one of the locals he frequented. So what was he up to when he deliberately lost any trackers who might be on his tail?

And then there was Bert Thatch.

He usually managed to get a corner of the pub to himself because of the peculiar odour that surrounded him. It had been likened to a combination of incontinent cats and ancient fish heads. It was probably the result of his diet, since he tended to make a living by grubbing through black plastic bin liners stacked outside the city restaurants and consuming whatever was edible and not too ripe before the garbage collectors made their rounds. He wore a matted beard and a motheaten, threadbare overcoat. His knuckles were encased in woollen gloves the fingers of which had been worn away. In drunken moments he claimed to be an eccentric millionaire. Oddly enough he never cadged drinks, but paid his own way—in moments of bonhomie he had even been known to buy a round. He was in such a mood at The Hydraulic Engine on Friday evening, when he buttonholed Jackie Parton. The ex-jockey resisted the odour only momentarily because Bert Thatch seemed to know something Jackie did not.

'Well, wor Jackie, not gettin' far with that lawyer friend of yourn, hey? I mean, that Cullen laddie that's been locked up, don't stand much chance, does he? Not while Ferdy Newton keeps close.'

Jackie stared at the old man, frowning. 'Keeps close? What do you mean?'

'All but gone to ground, hasn't he, the cunnin' old bugger. Oh, still doin' his rounds for Sam Turriff and all that but nervy as a hen on a hot china egg if you ask me.'

Parton hesitated. Casually he said, 'You seen him around, then?'

Bert Thatch chuckled. 'Duckin' here, duckin' there, if you know what I mean.'

'Ducking exactly *where*, Bert?'

Bert Thatch scratched at his matted beard and attempted a solemn face. 'Buy you a drink, Jackie, then I'll tell you. Not too many talk to me in here, you know. That bugger over there, polishin' the glasses—' he gestured towards the barman—'he thinks I'm bad for trade. Spend my money, don't I?' Leering, he ambled up to the bar, shouted at the barman when he was ignored, and then returned with two pints of beer. He wiped a stiff-coated arm across his nose, took a deep draught, and sighed. 'Now, where was I?'

'Ferdy Newton.'

'Ah yes. Funny business, that. Didn't you ask yerself, wor Jackie, what that bloody little ticket-man was doing out by the staiths? I asked myself at the time. Talk is he shopped this Cullen lad, but I ask you, hinny, what was *Ferdy* doin' out there?'

'His rounds,' Jackie said shortly, and sipped his beer.

Bert Thatch cackled. 'Rounds? He got no punters down at the staiths! You imagine Sam Turriff payin' out to the kind of drop-outs that squat in them rooms? Use your head, man!'

'He hasn't got any punters in that area?'

'Come on, Jackie! I thought you knew Tyneside. Who on that bank of the river is goin' to be credit-worthy enough for Sam Turriff? They's skaggies down there, squatters, meths men—give 'em a quid and they'd drink it or sniff it or inject it and never give a damn if they get slung in the river. There's no *custom* for Ferdy Newton down that way, man!'

He was right. The annoying thing was, Bert Thatch was right. It was so obvious: Jackie Parton cursed himself for not asking the question himself earlier, putting the case to Eric Ward.

'So what was Ferdy doing down at the staiths?' he asked Bert Thatch.

'Ain't up my sleeve,' the old man replied. 'Can't tell you. But he's behavin' very funny. I seen him, and he's hoppin' about like he thinks the Mounties is on his backside.'

The two occasions he had given Jackie the slip . . .

'Just where,' Jackie Parton asked slowly, 'just where was it you saw Ferdy, Bert?'

The old man picked up his pint, took a long slow pull at it, pouring the beer down his scrawny throat in one long swallow. He put down the glass, belched loudly and grinned at Jackie. 'Where? Well, I'll tell you. But it'll cost you, wor Jackie. A beer.' He grinned again, gap-toothed. 'Or two.'

Jackie Parton picked up Eric Ward at lunch-time. There was little chance that they would allow Ferdy Newton to slip away at this point for the ticket-man was ensconced in The Prince Albert and if he were true to form would remain there until three in the afternoon. He had had a busy morning along the South Shields manor: he had punters, it would seem, in the area running from Frenchman's Lea to

Corporation Quay. Now it was refreshment in The Prince Albert, which gave Jackie time to drive back the fifteen miles to the Quayside office to pick up Eric Ward.

'It's a bit odd,' Jackie commented as they crossed Byker Bridge and drove along the busy streets abutting Shields Road, 'that Ferdy Newton seems to have suddenly picked up the Frenchman's Lea patch. I mean, I been following him for a week now and all his punters have been in the West End and across the river in Gateshead. Twice he gives me the slip—and I think deliberately. Even if he didn't really know for certain he had a tail on him. And now he's busy around the Shields area.'

'Maybe Turriff's given him a new book,' Eric suggested.

'Likely. But in a sense it ties in with what Bert Thatch told me yesterday. Gets around, does Bert: God knows what he does apart from root in dustbins, but he gets around. And he reckons he was up at South Shields the other day and saw our friend Ferdy hopping about like a bear with a sore backside, doing his best not to be seen.'

'Where in Shields?'

'Corporation Quay. Or, to be more precise, just north of there at the landing-stage in Shields Harbour.'

'Which is where we're going now?' Eric asked.

'Not exactly. I got a feeling. We'll try the north shore, rather than South Shields.'

'Why?'

Jackie Parton was silent for a moment as he swung left to head for Hunters Quay and the river road east, and then he shrugged. 'Look at it this way, Mr Ward. I don't know what Ferdy's up to. As Bert Thatch said, what was he doing out at the staiths when Lister was killed: how come he *happened* to be there to see Cullen? And now, when he's in the middle of his ticket rounds, how come he suddenly changes his patch, and disappears every so often? I don't *know* what's going on, but I'd like to find out, and I got a hunch there's a connection somewhere in all this.'

Eric glanced out of the window towards the old Hebburn

Ferry landing-stage as the car turned into the river road. 'That still doesn't explain why we take the north shore, while Ferdy is drinking in a South Shields pub.'

'Near the landing-stage, Mr Ward. Think of it this way. Ferdy's been scuttling around like a frightened crab. He's got his eyes open wide. I've been pretty careful tracking him and I'm sure he hasn't seen me, but he's still nervous enough to give me the slip successfully. That betokens a *very* careful man. So now he's on the Frenchman's Lea patch. He goes to The Prince Albert. *If* he's going to jump sideways now —and he's in the area where Bert Thatch saw him nervous as a cat—he'd want to be sure he's not being followed.'

'So?'

'Around Corporation Quay it's pretty open. The quayside doesn't do much business now since Redheads Shipyard folded. The streets are pretty open, and quiet. Wherever Ferdy's going, he'd pick out anyone following him, easy as pie. But there's an even better bet, in my mind.'

'What's that?'

'Easiest way to drop someone—or locate them—would be to use the landing-stage. The ferry's a small one. Maybe Ferdy's not really interested in sticking to the south shore at all. He'll want to be across the river—but slipping any cover. There's no way, if I was trailing him, that I could get on that ferry without being spotted by him.'

'It's a long shot, Jackie, assuming he's coming to the north shore.'

Parton smiled. 'Not exactly, Mr Ward. Bert Thatch actually saw him board. I was just rationalizing. It's a pretty safe bet that Ferdy will leave The Prince Albert and take the North Shields ferry—'

'The Market Place ferry,' Eric amended.

The ex-jockey laughed. 'Hey, you been doing your own homework, Mr Ward!'

'It pays, occasionally,' Eric replied, smiling.

To their right now, as they passed through Willington Quay and the entrance to the Tyne Tunnel, the river swung black and wide past the wasteland of derricks rusting in the sun, to tumble past Albert Edward Dock and Coble Dene into Shields Harbour. Across the river Eric could see the remnants of what had once been a thriving industry: High Docks, West Docks, Middle Docks, running up to the dry dock at Brigham before the Tyne swung east again past the North Shields jetty and into the open sea. As he watched he could see a freighter, fluttering a Norwegian flag, negotiating The Narrows behind the pilot boat. Then the river was lost to sight as they dipped down the hill along Howdon Road and skirted Bull Ring Docks to drive into Duke Street and the landing-stage beyond at Market Place.

The river was busy. The Norwegian freighter, rust red in her hull, was now level with Brigham Dry Dock and being fussed around by the pilot boat and two small tugs trying to make their escape to the North Sea. At the Tyne Commission Quay Station a grey corvette idled, waiting for clearance papers and two small yachts fluttered their way into the harbour, red and blue sails reflected in the dark water. At the landing-stage there were a few cars parked and a small knot of people waiting for the ferry, women mainly, probably returning from the fish quay. A group of boys sat on the jetty, rods and lines waving as they sought the catch of their lifetimes that would never come.

Jackie Parton turned left into the hill and parked on a piece of waste land. He turned off the engine, and reached back to the rear of the car for a pair of powerful binoculars. 'You learn something in the racing business,' he said. 'If you want to know what's going on out there on the race-course, get the best glasses. These are a reminder of the old days, but they still come in useful.' He nudged Eric's arm. 'There. She's coming.'

From where they sat in the car they could see the landing-stage near the mercantile marine offices on the south shore. The ferry boat was small, self-important in its chugging progress, turning with the tide and swinging left before it picked up its diagonal run, north across the river to the landing-stage and the market place below Eric and Jackie Parton. The ex-jockey adjusted the binoculars and stared at the approaching ferry. There were no more than a dozen people aboard.

'Can you make him out?' Eric asked after a little while.

'Not sure.' Jackie lowered the glasses. 'Bit far off yet, but we'll know in a matter of minutes whether he's aboard or not.'

But it wasn't that easy. The ferry chugged doggedly across the river but the angle of its approach was such that it was impossible to distinguish the people who stood on the open deck. Only when it came broadside on to manœuvre up to the landing-stage did the passengers become more clearly identifiable.

Ferdy Newton was not among them.

Jackie Parton swore under his breath. He kept his eyes glued to the glasses as the ferryboat berthed and the passengers began to come ashore. The waiting group began to mingle with them, elbowing their way aboard impatiently, and the group became indistinct, swirling around the narrow confines of the landing-stage. Then Jackie Parton swore again.

'What is it?' Eric asked.

'Cunning bugger. There he is. He's been in the wheel-house. Keeping under cover.'

He handed the binoculars to Eric. Adjustments were needed to the focus: Eric was reminded that his own eyesight could hardly match the ex-jockey's. When he finally made the adjustment he had difficulty picking out the gangway. When he did, it was to see Ferdy Newton shuffling along it on to the landing-stage. He walked in an almost parody of furtiveness.

'He's going carefully.'

'Canny lad.'

Jackie Parton retrieved the binoculars and fixed on Newton again. Eric waited. He could barely make out the man at this distance and indeed lost him twice in the movement down at the landing-stage. It was almost two minutes before Newton moved away.

'He's being canny all right,' Parton said softly. 'He's just about sussed out everyone within thirty yards. But he's moving now, and at a fair pace.'

'Where's he headed?'

Jackie Parton was silent for a little while, straining intently to keep the ticket-man in sight. Then he lowered the binoculars with a satisfied sigh. 'One thing's for certain, he's not chasing up any punters.'

'How do you mean?'

'He's going into Bull Ring Docks.'

Parton turned on the engine, and drove the car down the hill to park it near the landing-stage in Duke Street. 'If he'd gone up there among the terraces, we could well have lost him,' he commented. 'But in Bull Ring Docks . . .'

'What's in there now?' Eric asked.

Parton locked the car and turned to face him. He squinted up to Eric in the afternoon sunshine and shrugged. 'Nothing,' he said.

'So let's go see what Ferdy Newton's up to in there.'

The old graving docks had been allowed to decay and rust away in the face of the death of the industry along the Tyne. Attempts at revival had been desultory and were now completely abandoned. The iron-gated entrance had been imposing but was now a hulk, rusty iron sagging on broken hasps. The large stone-slabbed driveway was pitted and weed-littered; graffiti of an uninspiring and repetitive kind defaced the old stone walls of the roofless buildings and the whole area had the odour of discontent about it, a desperation at being neglected, a knowledge that there was nothing left.

The yards were silent. Eric and Jackie Parton moved quietly, and watchfully. They had caught a glimpse of Newton towards the far end of the graving dock as he had turned left into a narrow alleyway between some old offices and now they moved carefully across the broken ground, anxious not to disturb him before they were able to discover what he was up to.

At the alleyway entrance they paused. The alley was littered with refuse and stalked by a ginger cat, intent on a nonchalant seagull perched on a block of fallen masonry. They stood there for a few minutes, not knowing how to proceed, for the alleyway ended against a high stone wall topped with barbed wire: an ineffective and dated attempt to keep the yards clear of vandals. The door of one of the offices yawned brokenly open: Newton could have gone in there, but they could not be sure.

'What now?' Jackie Parton asked.

The afternoon was silent about them, sounds of the town two hundred yards away lost among the broken walls of the old graving dock. Gulls planed high above their heads, drifting on wind eddies above the dark waters of the Tyne, and the ginger cat turned its attention away from the bird on the stone to watch the two men with a baleful stare, ready to spring into flight if they moved.

Eric moved, and the cat leaped away, scrabbling incredibly up the stone wall and ducking under the barbed wire. Parton followed Eric as he walked down into the alleyway.

Something clattered inside the hallway of the old office at the end of the alley. Eric reached the broken door: inside the light was dim, dirt-encrusted windows letting in only minimum light. But the dust on the floor had been disturbed; it hung lazily in the stray shafts of sunlight that entered through the open door.

Eric moved inside, Jackie Parton just behind him. The hallway was small enough, with three doorways leading off it. None boasted a door: the wood had been taken long ago, perhaps for firewood, perhaps for sliding down wasteland slopes. The air was fusty and dust-laden, the odour one of decay.

'Newton?' Eric called. 'Ferdy Newton?'

If flight had been possible, Newton no doubt would have taken to flight. But there was no other entrance or exit, it would seem, and after a short interval there was a scuffling sound and Ferdy Newton appeared in the doorway of one of the small offices.

He stood there blinking. He seemed shrunken with nervousness, and his hands were shaking as he stared at them, black against the light in the doorway. The braggart confidence he had displayed when first Eric had met him had gone: now he was hunched with fear, and trembling. He could hardly raise his head and he put out one shaking hand to the wall for support. He tried to say something, but his tone was strangled.

'What the hell are you doing here, Newton?' Eric asked.

Something happened to the ticket-man at the sound of Eric's voice. He raised his head, suspiciously, but the suspicion changed to relief. He straightened, peered at the two men as though he had not recognized them before and the trembling slowed, stopped; he stood away from the wall, still crouching and glared at Eric and Jackie Parton.

'Ward!' He almost spat out the word. 'You followed me here!'

'That's right. We've been curious, you see, to discover just what you've been up to.'

'I got nothing of interest for you.'

'That may be so. But I still think we need to have a chat.'

'I got nothing to say.'

'Not even about Cullen?'

Ferdy Newton sneered. His confidence was returning, oddly, but it was still underscored by a certain nervousness. He began to move forward, almost sliding against the wall, wanting to leave this place.

'Cullen will get what he deserved, for sticking Eddie Lister. I've said all I'm going to say. And now I'm leaving.'

'No,' Eric said firmly. 'Not yet. I don't know why you've been skulking around this graving dock and I don't much care: your dirty little business is your own affair. But you've got some questions to answer. About Liam Geraghty, and Peter Maxwell and the kidnapping of Kate Cullen.'

'I don't know what the hell you're talking about!'

'Then maybe I can sketch in a few perspectives for you. There was a curious public-spiritedness about your phoning the police to link Tony Cullen to the scene of Lister's death. It was out of character. You even gave your name to the police.'

'I told you. He almost ran me down. I was mad. Now I'm getting out of here.'

Jackie Parton moved. He stood in the doorway. A small man, he was nevertheless, even since his retirement from the turf, tough and wiry. Ferdy Newton, pot-bellied, eyed him warily.

'You're not going anywhere, Ferdy, until you've answered my questions,' Eric said softly. 'You told the police Tony Cullen almost ran you down. Were you the one who also phoned—anonymously—to tell them someone had been murdered at the staiths blocks?'

'You look here, Ward—'

'Because we've started to link things together, Ferdy. You had no real reason to be at the staiths—'

'My book—'

'You've got no punters down there,' Parton said quietly. Ferdy Newton was silent for a few moments, his glance darting nervously between Eric and Jackie Parton. 'So what were you doing down there, Ferdy?' Eric asked. 'Perhaps it was *you* who stuck that knife into Eddie Lister.'

'Oh no, you're not nailing me with that one,' Newton said viciously. 'They got Cullen, and I saw him down there, and I'll testify and there's damn-all you can do about it.'

'I'm not sure your testimony will hold water when we explain about Geraghty and Maxwell,' Eric said.

'Geraghty, Geraghty, what the hell is all this about? I got no idea what you're talking about!'

'Then I'll spell it out for you. You get around, you hear what's going on. After Lister was knifed you worked out a little plan that would leave you with cash in your pocket. Maybe you *did* see Cullen down at the staiths—maybe you just heard he was there. Whichever way it was, you thought that if Cullen was hauled in by the police there was a way you could profit by it. You knew his daughter had been kidnapped; you'd heard Geraghty was behind it. You approached him—or Peter Maxwell—and put it forward. You'd testify against Cullen, get him put away, for a cash payment. Maxwell would go along with that: it would remove Cullen, get him out of the way while the removal of Kate Cullen went on.'

'Maxwell? I never even heard of Maxwell!'

'You hear a great deal on your ticket rounds. You'll have heard that Maxwell made contact with Chad Cowell through a business contract, and that through Cowell he got hold of Eddie Lister, to act as strongarm man in the kidnapping. And you thought you could get in on the money, offer your services to two men who'd be prepared to pay for it.'

'You're crazy!' Newton almost spat out the words as he edged crablike along the wall, easing his way towards the door. 'All this talk about Geraghty and Maxwell and Lister is crazy! I didn't get involved with any of that. I don't *know* Maxwell. And I never been in touch with Geraghty. And now I want to get out of here.'

'Before Maxwell—or one of his contacts—arrives to pay you off, Ferdy?' Parton asked. 'I mean, why else are you skulking around down here? You're here to meet someone, of course. And you took great care not to be seen. Is this where the whole thing was negotiated, between you and Maxwell or Geraghty?'

'I tell you I don't know what you're talking about! Now let me get out of—'

A cat yowled in the alleyway and there was a scrambling sound, a tin turning and clattering, and a muffled curse. The sound snapped off Ferdy Newton's protest and he stood stiffly with his back to the wall, eyes wide. Eric stared at him: the man had been nervous and sweating, shaking in his eagerness to leave the building. But it wasn't fear that riveted him now; rather, there was a desperation in his eyes, a droop of resignation to his flabby mouth that puzzled Eric. Jackie Parton moved silently away from the door, gesturing to Eric to step aside also.

'Ferdy?'

The man was a matter of feet from the doorway and Newton tried to say something but his mouth was dry. The three of them stood there in the dim light, staring at the doorway, waiting. Then he appeared, slouching, haggard.

'Ferdy?'

There was a pause. He stared into the dimness questioningly. He saw Ferdy Newton standing against the wall, the two men standing close by and his hand reached backwards, to the belt he wore under his coarse duffel jacket. There was a click, the blade slipping out of the sprung handle. A shaft of sunlight caught the bright blade, gave it life.

'Chad? You come to get yours have you, Chad? Well, here it is, you bastard!'

3

Ferdy Newton had sagged against the wall, but now he came upright, hands held out half pleadingly, half defensively. 'Now hold it, for God's sake! Put that bloody thing away!'

The young man's thin body was tensed, his deep-set eyes glaring as he stood in the doorway. His hand was extended with the knife, scarred veins standing out darkly against his translucent skin. 'Ferdy? They got you here, Ferdy?'

'I tell you, put that damned knife away! And get the hell out of here!'

'Naw. Done enough runnin'. It's time I stopped and gave the bastards what I gave Lister.'

There was a short silence, broken only by the wheezing gasp of despair that came from a sagging-faced Ferdy Newton. Eric Ward stepped forward in the dim light of the old office and stared at the young man with the knife. He knew him.

'Phil? Phil Heckles? *You* killed Eddie Lister?'

There was a bluish tinge about the sharp cheekbones and there was nothing in the glazed eyes to suggest Heckles had recognized Eric Ward. The knife was still held out menacingly, and there was no shake in the fingers. Something moved in Eric's stomach when he realized that the man was high, probably on heroin. With the realization came the memory of something someone had said, days ago.

'Yeh, I killed the bastard,' Phil Heckles said confidently. 'And now I've got you here, now you've finally caught up with me, I'm going to stick you too.'

'Phil, for God's sake,' Ferdy Newton pleaded, 'Chad Cowell's not here!'

'Always said, when I go I'll go in style,' Heckles said menacingly, ignoring Ferdy Newton's protest. 'And for me, style was getting you bastards screaming up and down the Tyne. That safe house in Chester-le-Street, you never really thought it *was* safe, did you? Any of the skaggies in the West End could tell you about the safe houses you stupid bastards were using. And it was so easy. Nobody else had the guts to cross a runner, but I did. And easy it was. I saw the stuff planted, and I just walked in, lifted it, and you was nowhere in sight! But you didn't half start screamin' after that!'

Eric recalled the gossip in the courtroom from the barrister Eldon Samuels; police embarrassment at the failure of their operation to arrest the dealers who were expecting a shipment of heroin from Teesside Airport. The safe house in Chester-le-Street; the traffic accident on the A1; the dealer being confounded on *his* arrival at the house to find someone had beaten him to it.

'You lifted the drugs from Chester-le-Street?' Eric asked.

'Don't say nothin',' Ferdy Newton pleaded.

Eric stared at the ticket-man, puzzled, then turned back to Heckles, still menacing with the knife. 'Phil—'

'Back off,' the young man said. 'Come close and you'll

get it in the gut! I'm telling you, Cowell, I lifted it, like you heard, but if you thought you could simply put your muscle on me and get the skag back, you were wrong. I dumped most of it on the street within days—even *gave* it away. All I wanted was to get the boot into you and the bloody barons behind you! And I did it, me, Phil Heckles, I did it! And when that big bastard Lister caught up with me, I did for him too! Like I'm going to carve you, now!'

'Phil, listen to me,' Eric said quietly. 'Chad Cowell isn't here. You remember me. Eric Ward. I acted for you in court. I'm a solicitor . . . I came to see you at Jacob Holyoake Street.'

Where Ferdy Newton had been hanging around, and had warned Eric to stay away from Heckles. And Newton had been at the staiths when Heckles had knifed Lister. As he was here now, meeting Heckles, worried about being followed . . . by Chad Cowell. Eric's mind surged over the puzzle but this was no time to concentrate on it. Heckles hardly seemed to have heard Eric's words, let alone understood them. He was in a half crouch, his knife arm tense, and he took a slow, cautious step forward, his hollow eyes fixed and staring at Eric. Ferdy Newton stepped forward, pleading again. 'Listen to me, Phil. What he said is true. Chad Cowell isn't here. I was careful, made sure none of Cowell's mob was following me. How the hell Ward and that little bastard over there tracked me I don't know, but they got nothing to do with Cowell. It's the bloody solicitor, Ward, and you got to get away from here while you still can.'

The plea had not registered on Heckles. The addict was still glaring through a drug-induced haze at Eric, the focus of his hate, and he was brushing Ferdy aside. 'Don't worry, Ferdy. I got the bastard in my sights. I've crawled to him for years, and he's treated me like muck. But I screwed him good, and he's had the barons on his neck, and he's had to pay up and now he's going to pay me. With his blood!'

'Phil—'

The word was almost a wail, as everything seemed to happen at once. Jackie Parton had remained behind Eric, and to his left. Now as Heckles moved forward, swiftly, with his knife extended towards Eric, Parton leaped across the intervening space, reaching for the knife arm. Panicked, squealing, Ferdy Newton threw himself forward to block the attack, tripping up the ex-jockey and sending him sprawling sideways. But Heckles had been thrown off balance too, and Eric grabbed at his arm, pulling, so that the young addict came crashing forward, helplessly, flailing the knife wildly in the air. Eric had two hands clasped on the wrist, beating it against his knee, and Heckles's left hand hammered ineffectually at Eric's shoulder. Jackie Parton was down, sprawling, but struggling to rise, and Ferdy Newton came rushing at Eric, his tubby body charging into the two struggling men. He crashed into Eric, thrust him against the wall, and as Eric's grip loosened Heckles tore himself free.

'Get out . . .' Newton gasped. 'Get the hell out of here!'

But it was too late. Half-crazed, excited by the action and surging with hate for the dealer he was still convinced was facing him, Heckles came again, thrusting hard with the knife.

'*Phil!*' Ferdy Newton screamed the word as he tried to block the thrust. He tried to scream again, but the sound was cut off in his throat as he took the punching movement of the knife in his body, interposed between Eric and Heckles. He grabbed at the young man's shoulders, falling forward and shouting in shock, and at last something seemed to get through to Phil Heckles. He halted, half supporting Newton, staring down at the man as he lurched to his knees, doubling forward, clutching at his chest. Heckles began to shudder, started to say something as the bubbling words came from Ferdy Newton's panicked lips. 'Aw, bloody hell, Phil, bloody hell . . .'

The tone was not anger, but despair and resignation, even as the blood seeped blackly through his fingers. Phil Heckles stared down at him, and the knife clattered to the stone floor. He put out a questioning hand, touched Newton's shoulder, and then his face crumpled.

'Ferdy . . .'

Eric leaned back against the wall, breathing hard, and something Nick Hawthorne had told him came seeping back into his mind. Ferdy Newton was a petty criminal, but he had always had one saving grace.

And he had had a half-brother who had once worked on the rigs.

4

The prosecution of Sam Turriff was scheduled for the Tuesday. Eric and Nick Hawthorne had every confidence it would be successful, and the Office of Fair Trading had for once acted with despatch and revoked Turriff's trading licence. At the weekend Eric was able to relax, walking in the woods above Sedleigh Hall with Anne, in a hazy, pale afternoon sunshine. Black grouse cackled on the moorland above them, and down at the river he could see banks of rosebay willow herb spreading a splash of colour, reflected in the water.

'So,' Anne said, linking her arm through his. 'That man Newton is off the critical list?'

'Seems so. The knife missed his lung by a fraction, but he'll survive.'

'To face charges?'

'Quite a few. Not least, accessory after the fact to murder.'

'Newton wasn't really *involved* with the whole thing, though, was he?'

Eric shook his head. 'Not really. What happened was that Phil Heckles, wanting to go out in his sick little blaze of glory, intercepted Chad Cowell's heroin drop. Once Heckles started to unload the heroin on Tyneside streets it was just a matter of time before Cowell learned who had raided the

Chester-le-Street safe house. He set his thug Lister on to the problem. Lister discovered where Heckles was hiding out and went after him. But Ferdy Newton was there, too.'

'He took part in the killing?'

'Apparently not. For all his loud talk, Ferdy Newton is just a little ticket-man who doesn't like to get involved personally in violence. It seems Lister burst in, went for Heckles and got a knife in his stomach for his trouble. Ferdy just danced around in desperation and then bundled Phil Heckles out of there, to get him away to a new hideout, down at Bull Ring Docks in South Shields.'

'But he'd seen Cullen at the staiths.'

'That's right,' Eric agreed. 'And he saw a way to cover for his half-brother. He phoned in—anonymously—to tell the police there'd been a killing. Then, riskily, he phoned again, leaving his name this time, to fix Cullen at the scene, through the use of the Chaddha car.'

'And then, at Bull Ring Docks he turned up again—still looking after Heckles?'

Eric nodded. 'Heckles was high on heroin. Ferdy was going to the docks to make sure he was keeping low, and was all right. But Heckles was so hazed by the drug he thought I was Chad Cowell—certainly his knifing of Ferdy Newton was accidental.'

'He was trying to knife *you*,' Anne expostulated.

'He was drugged to the eyeballs. Hardly knew what he was doing.'

'And you had no idea, then, that Newton and Heckles were half-brothers?'

Eric shook his head. 'How could I? Well . . . maybe I *should* have made the connection. I mean, Newton turned up at Jacob Holyoake Street, protective as ever of his family, and warned me away from Heckles. And Nick Hawthorne at the DHSS had indeed told me all about Newton's protectiveness—and the fact that Newton had had a half-brother who had worked on the rigs. I knew it was on the rigs that Heckles had first picked up the habit. But they were facts I hadn't put together. I was concentrating on other things . . .'

'Like Tony Cullen, and the charges against him.'

'That's right.' They turned along the pathway that led through dappled undergrowth until they came out on top of the rise. The moorland fell away in front of them and the Cheviot appeared mistily through the afternoon haze, its slopes fading away greyly in the distance.

'The police will be embarrassed about having to release Cullen,' Anne suggested.

'More than that. I was talking to my gossiping friend Eldon Samuels in court yesterday. He tells me all hell has broken loose at Morpeth. I must say I did try to warn Mason but he wasn't prepared to listen. The fact is, now that the case against Cullen has blown up in his face he's been suspended from duty. He might have thought he'd get the support of his chiefs but in the event they've pulled the rug from under him. His conduct of the Cullen case has been called into account and they've started investigating the way in which he's handled the kidnapping of Kate, as well.'

'But some of the higher-ups will have been *involved* in that cover-up!' Anne said indignantly.

'True, but they'll be hurrying to find a scapegoat. Mason is it. Oh, I don't think they'll get away with it entirely. Some of the mud will stick and there'll be red faces and bad publicity for a number of people, from the Lord Lieutenant and the Chief Constable downwards. There are times when even money can't cover the truth.'

'Geraghty's money, you mean?' Anne frowned. 'What happens to him now?'

'There's a warrant out for him. And Samuels tells me that Peter Maxwell was about to leave for New York this weekend but has had his passport confiscated.'

'They can show he was involved in the kidnapping of Kate Cullen?'

Eric nodded. 'We've always guessed that Geraghty was

involved. Now Mason's been set up as a scapegoat, it seems there's enough proof crawling out of the woodwork to show Geraghty *did* set up the kidnapping, financially. Maxwell—well, I was on the wrong tack when I thought there was some connection between him and Ferdy Newton—but he certainly made use of his acquaintance with Chad Cowell to get the use of the man with the scarred nose. And now Davinia O'Hara's been pulled in she's getting treatment for her addiction and confirming all sorts of things. Not least that Lister made the snatch, and Peter Maxwell was driving. She identified him in a line-up. He drove the car because they thought his presence—a familiar face—would help calm Kate down a little once she was grabbed.'

'So Lister did the grabbing, went back about his business with Cowell in Sunderland—'

'And Geraghty arranged passage for Kate to Ireland, and then to the States. Geraghty and Maxwell will get indicted.'

'And Chad Cowell?'

'Not as far as the kidnapping is concerned. But,' Eric explained, 'Davinia O'Hara's a key witness against him. She will testify she got drugs from Cowell at the Windmill Leisure Centre, along with other young people. And there's Heckles too: he hates Cowell and now he's under arrest for murder he'll be giving testimony enough to put Cowell inside on a major drugs charge.'

'Hmmm. Is there any chance Geraghty will buy himself off the charges against him?' Anne asked doubtfully.

'Unlikely. Kidnapping is regarded seriously by the English courts—even if the kidnapper is the child's grandfather.'

'That still leaves the problem of Kate.'

Eric was silent for a while, as they turned and walked back down through the shadowed footpath and across the yellowing fields towards Sedleigh Hall. He recalled Tony Cullen's release from police custody. He had met him in Durham, walked with him through the narrow streets of the city, climbed the hill to the cathedral and stood with him looking at the great loop of the river as it meandered below the ancient walls of city and castle and cathedral. He remembered Cullen's tortured conversation, his indecision. And the words of the ophthalmic surgeon had come back to Eric. A blurred reality. Perhaps Eric Ward and Tony Cullen had both suffered from the same failure to perceive the truly significant.

'The fact is, in a marriage like Cullen and Geraghty's daughter had, in the end there's no black and white. There's no base for truth any more: once sides are taken, fact becomes distorted by changing viewpoints. When Cullen told me his story, it was *his* side of it, inevitably. Geraghty tried to put Ruth's case, and maybe I was too involved with it all at that stage to listen properly. There was fault on both sides. And after Ruth went to the States, I think Cullen allowed his pride to get the better of Kate's need.'

'But even so . . .'

'Don't get me wrong,' Eric said. 'It's true Cullen can get an extradition order to have his daughter returned to him from the States. Once the story gets out he's bound to get a great deal of public sympathy. There'll be financial support flooding in to help him—'

'*We* could help,' Anne said firmly. 'And I think we *should* help.'

'But it's not that simple. I talked to Cullen at Durham. He's undecided. He knows there's little enough he can do for Kate. In the States, Ruth will be able to give the youngster a comfortable life. Cullen loves his daughter but the realities of which he's become convinced over the years are now blurred. He questions, rightly, whether in trying to get Kate back he's merely indulging himself at her expense. Maybe he should let things alone, not struggle any longer.

'But *kidnapping*!'

'I know. The guilty need to be punished. And that includes Ruth Geraghty. But *Kate* is an innocent in all this. What about her? What's *best* for her?'

Anne was silent for a little while, subdued. Then she

sighed. 'You've decided, as far as you're concerned, haven't you?'

'What should be done? Yes, I guess so.'

'So what advice have you given Cullen?'

'I've told him he shouldn't give up the struggle, but he should re-direct it. Whatever the rights and wrongs of the whole situation, both Cullen and Ruth Geraghty probably want what's best for Kate. They should both be made to realize that. And instead of *fighting* to get what's best for her, they need to get together, talk about it, reach a rational, agreeable solution. If the courts are brought into it there's little doubt what *they'll* do. Custody to Tony Cullen again, maintenance to be paid by Ruth. But I've advised Cullen he shouldn't let it come to that. He's got to see Ruth, got to meet her, so they can talk things through properly, and reach an amicable agreement.'

'You think it can be done?'

'I think it *will* be done,' Eric said firmly. 'Everyone in this issue has suffered trauma, scars. But it can all be resolved, if they simply consider the main issue: Kate's happiness . . .'

And then, he thought, perhaps the realities might emerge from behind the fogs of blind emotion, and even the kidnapping of Kate Cullen would have made some sense, in the end.